P9-CMW-750

ON MY HONOUR

ELIZABETH JOHNS

To Those Who Gave All

Copyright © 2019 by Elizabeth Johns
Cover Design by 17 Studio Book Design
and Wilette Youkey
Edited by Heather King

ISBN-13: 978-0-9965754-9-2

All rights reserved.
No part of this book may be reproduced in any form or by any electronic or mechanical
means, including information storage and retrieval systems, without written
permission from the author, except for the use of brief quotations in a book review.

BRETHREN IN ARMS PROLOGUE

Vitoria, Northern Spain, June 1813
The Allied Encampment

*T*he grief was so thick in their throats, none could speak. They had been together for only two years, yet the bonds of the battle were forged stronger than any created by blood. It was not something that could be explained, only experienced.

When they had set sail from England for the Peninsula, each had felt invincible, ready to conquer evil and save England. Now, it was hard to remember why they needed to be brave any more.

There was a chill in the air as they all sat huddled around the fire. James shivered. The silence the night before a battle was eerie, but afterwards, it was deafening. Watching the campfire's flames perform their blue, gold and orange dance, it did not seem real that one of them was gone. They had survived Ciudad Rodrigo, Badajoz, and Salamanca, yet Peter had fallen before their eyes today. His sabre had been raised and his eyes fierce, ready to charge when a shot had seared through him. He was on his horse one moment and gone the next. The scene replayed over and over in their minds in slow-motion. Memory was a cruel, cruel master. The same battle had left Luke wounded when a shell exploded near him. He had insisted on joining them tonight, eschewing the orders of the sawbones and hobbling out of the medical tent on the arm of his batman, Tobin.

Now, there were six of them left, if Peter's widow was included, and all wondered, *Was this to be their fate?*

Someone had to speak and break the chain of their morbid, damning thoughts.

"Peter would not want this." Four pairs of morose eyes looked up at Matthias. "We all knew this was likely when we signed up to fight Napoleon."

"How would you want us to feel if it were you?" James asked.

"I would want you to keep going and give my life meaning."

"Precisely. We mourn this night and move forward tomorrow. His death shall not be in vain," James said with quiet conviction.

"I still do not understand how we were caught unawares. Unless…" Colin was replaying the scene over in his mind.

"Someone gave our position away." Luke voiced what they all suspected.

"We were ambushed," Matthias added. In the end, England had emerged the victor, but it had been a near thing.

"What about Kitty?" Peter's wife followed the drum and felt like one of them.

"We see what she wishes to do. I expect she will wish to return home," Matthias answered. He had known her and Peter from the cradle and was the most devastated by the loss.

"The French are worn down; this cannot go on much longer," Luke said, though he would be sent home. No one else dared voice such hope.

"We are worn down," James muttered.

Philip, the quiet, thoughtful one, spoke. "If anything happens to me, will someone look to my sister? She has no one else."

"I swear it," Colin said, leading the others to do the same.

"*Pietas et honos.*"

Philip nodded, too affected to speak.

"Loyalty and honour." Another swore the oath in English.

They returned to silence, each brooding over what had happened and what was yet to come.

CHAPTER 1

January 1814

*L*uke walked along the Portsmouth pier to clear his head despite the cold, damp drizzle, happy to be on English soil once again after months in hospital with a festering wound. Though he would not trade the comradeship forged with his brothers in arms, he was grateful to be home, mostly whole, and now resolved to do his duty. Soldiers and sailors alike stumbled along the cobblestones in drunken revelry, the port full of public houses and taverns to tempt them to further libations. A great many of them had arrived home alongside him, invalided out of His Majesty's service. He made his way toward the George Inn, a fair place to rest before heading to London on the morrow, then on to his estate.

Pausing to relax his leg a moment, he leaned heavily on his cane and thought of Waverley, the place which had kept him going for the past two years while in the army. Not that he had expected to inherit, but his stupid cousin had found himself killed in a duel. His cousin had been insufferable (it was why he had been duelling in the first place), but he would not have wished for his death.

It was true, the notion that you do not appreciate what you have until it is gone. He had refused to leave the war upon inheriting, defying his superior's wishes, but what good was a title if there was nothing left to return to? Just because he had no heir...he had already tired of his responsibilities, and wanted to be treated as before, fighting for King and Country alongside his fellow man. War was certainly a great equalizer—a necessary one. He was more of a man now, maturity gained that would possibly have taken a lifetime to garner otherwise.

He scoffed aloud. If he ever heard any Johnny Raw discuss war as an adventure he would whip them soundly and save them a good deal of heartache. No one could have prepared him...he felt a lump in his throat at the thought and shook his head. So lost was he in grief that he almost stumbled over something in his path. Stopping abruptly, he peered through the murk. Some brawling drunks were blocking his way forward. When had he begun walking again? He could not recall. Clearing his throat, he hoped it was an innocent bout of fisticuffs.

"Pardon me?"

"Mind your own business," was the rude reply.

It was difficult to see what was happening through the dense fog, but Luke heard a whimper and it was distinctly feminine.

He felt for the handle of his cane, whilst leaning on his good leg to be ready to draw the sword out if needed. First, though, he tried his best command voice. "Step away from the woman so I can ensure she is willing." He heard another muffled plea, sounding like 'help'.

"We found 'er first," one of three men growled, and Luke pulled out his sword, leaving no doubt that he meant to protect the woman. Even if she was a ha' penny whore, she was protesting and that was enough for him.

"Step away from the lady."

"This ain't no lady." The short, dumpy one guffawed.

It would be three against one, but Luke had fared worse at Rodrigo...and Badajoz...and Salamanca...and it was no time for such remembrances. He needed his wits about him.

One of the men whispered to the other and Luke calculated. One would hold on to the woman and he suspected the other two would

6

try to take him from the sides. He waited for them to make the first move, which was not long in coming. Luke had to admire the bold approach. The largest one came for him head first, and Luke used the butt of his sword to knock him in the back of the head. That drill had been done hundreds of times with a sabre atop his battle horse, Trojan, but it was still gratifying with his sword.

The other man was small and wily, and Luke saw the flash of a dagger only seconds before it came down. He barely had time to balance and thrust before the dagger sliced into his thigh. Looking up as he pulled his sword out of the prone body, the woman was struggling with her captor. As the final man looked down at the fate of his fellow thug, she took the opportunity to place her knee in a spot which made Luke wince. However, he approved of her methods. The fool had made the mistake of looking over to see if he was next.

Luke quickly knocked the man senseless and trussed him like a Christmas goose before doing the same to the other two.

"Are you hurt, miss?"

She was breathing heavily and trembling, but he saw a slight shake of her head.

"Where may I escort you?"

"Nowhere," she whispered. Had they hurt her neck and injured her voice? He stepped closer and she flinched. She smelled foul, like the Thames at low tide. What had happened to her? Where had they found her?

"I will not harm you."

"You are bleeding, sir," she stated unexpectedly instead of female histrionics. Luke had forgotten about the dagger in his thigh. A similar thing had happened during the last battle and he had not noticed his injuries until much later, when the fire in his blood had settled. She did have a voice, however and it was that of a finely bred gentlewoman.

"A doctor should tend to this," she insisted, now fretting over him as though he had not just saved her from attack.

"My inn is not far from here. Is there somewhere I can escort you?" he asked again.

She shook her head with vehemence.

"Miss, I cannot leave you here alone after what has happened."

"We will not discuss myself when you are in danger of bleeding to death."

He sighed deeply. She was a stubborn one. "Very well. The George is up ahead, on Queen Street." Holding out his arm, he gave her a look his subalterns would have known well. She hesitated but then took it. He was afraid he would lean on her more than she on him. She was wet and shivering, and he could only speculate as to why the latter.

The distance to the inn had not seemed so far before. He could feel the blood trickling down his leg and pooling in his boot. By the time they stepped through the door, he was feeling very weak. Would that not be the worst bit of irony, to survive battle and die from a dagger in a dark alley in England?

"Please send for a doctor! My brother has been attacked." The miss ordered the landlord in the style of the highest lady in the land. In fact, she sounded much like his mother or sister.

He had little time to consider that fact before he was ushered into a parlour and a glass of spirits was held to his lips.

The lady fussed over him and cleaned his wounds. No female had done any fussing over him since his mother or nursemaid. It felt nice. He looked up at her through the haze of medicinal spirits and her face was hidden beneath her cloak, making her seem otherworldly. He felt a frown crease his forehead. "Is your rescuer not to know your name?"

"I am very grateful to you, sir, but I think it best if we remain nameless."

That was not the response he was used to hearing in England. A cold cloth was pressed to his forehead, and he could feel his leg throbbing beneath the makeshift tourniquet she had applied.

"Given names, then. I am Luke."

"Only between you and I?" She finally looked up at him enough so he could see her eyes, as pale as ice, and a small wisp of hair that looked like spun gold.

"Word of a gentleman."

Her gaze narrowed upon him and he could see she almost changed her mind. "I am Meg," she said at last, so quietly he barely heard.

"Meg," he whispered, as though the name was sacred. She smiled at him and he knew he would take a hundred more stab wounds to see it again.

He reached out and grazed his fingers along the bruise darkening on her cheek. Then he took his dampened handkerchief from his brow and held it to her wound. The tenderness in her eyes almost made him forget himself.

A knock on the door interrupted the intimacy, and his batman, Tobin, entered with the doctor—the dreaded sawbones.

"'Tis what happens when ye take the air," Tobin shook his head and muttered curses, before pouring enough whisky down his throat to sauce an entire regiment.

Luke's last coherent sentence to Meg was, "I will return you home after I am shewn up."

MEG WAITED IN A BEDROOM, and could hear the soldier's groans from the adjoining parlour while the doctor was sewing the cut. She felt horrible for leaving the man in such a state. In fact, she almost took the chance to stay until he was recovered. He was hurt because of her, after all, but she could not risk anyone discovering her. He was an officer and a gentleman, and his man and surgeon were seeing to him, so there was a little more she could do. He was in God's hands now. She would say prayers for her rescuer every day for the rest of her life. When she thought of what had almost happened at the hands of those vile ruffians, bile began to rise in her throat. She would have to learn how to repel such advances, though, since she was no longer to be a lady.

Adding sins to her guilt, she borrowed some coins from the gentleman who had been so kind to save her. One day, she would repay him, if it was the last thing she did. Leaving him a note of apology, she ripped off her locket and left it in exchange, since she had no idea where to pawn it. Offering a hasty prayer again that she was not taking from someone in need, she consoled herself that he had not seemed so. "Please let it be enough," she whispered, looking at the locket one last time.

Prying open the window, she looked down at the ground below. The room faced the stable-yard, and no one seemed to be about. It would not be long before her absence was discovered and they came looking for her. All she cared about now was getting as far away from Portsmouth and the vile Mr. Thurgood as was possible. There was a small wooden foothold over a door-case between her room and the ground, and she lowered herself to it. It was not easy to be a villain in skirts. Once steady, she made the final leap to the ground. It jarred her ankles, but the pain eased after a few moments. Now she only had to hide until Thurgood's ship set sail or she found transport away from this place. Could fortune smile upon her and her absence not be discovered until the ship was far out to sea? Ha! When she awoke on the ship and realized she had been drugged, she had pleaded illness and begged the servants to leave her undisturbed. Perhaps the after-effects of the drugs had made her bold, but her only thought had been to get away.

This time, she skirted the shadows until she was free of the town. Never again would she be caught unawares. It had not been dangerous to walk in her small village. There were no more lights to guide her way, and only a small slice of a moon. Her feet were beginning to ache, and she had probably only trudged a mile or two. How would she get all the way to Amelia? Not that she could simply arrive on Amelia's doorstep and expect an open welcome, but she knew she would help somehow. Meg needed to know her sister was happy. At least the man Amelia had been sold to would not take her to a faraway land.

"Can I help you, miss?"

Meg jumped with fright. Not again!

The older man held up his hands. "I mean you no harm but a young lady shouldn't be out here on her own in the middle of the night."

"You are correct, sir." She had to think of a plausible story, but there really was not one.

"Are you trying to run away?" he asked kindly.

"I suppose I am, in a manner of speaking. I was to be forced into a bad situation." She was afraid to say more. He was most likely about to drag her back to town, thinking her an errant wife.

"Where are you headed, then?"

If only Meg could remember the name. She only knew it was near Oxford, since her uncle had listed the large estate as one of the earl's qualities.

"North."

"I take a cart towards Basingstoke in the morning, if you don't mind the rough ride. You could catch the stage from there."

"I would be most grateful, sir."

"Come, get out of the cold. The missus will look after you." He indicated a small cottage set behind a hedge that she had not noticed from the road. He seemed genuinely concerned and was old enough to be her father. Hopefully she was not walking into another trap. Her parents must be turning in their graves. They had trusted Uncle Irving to look after Amelia and her; instead, he had sold both of them to the highest bidders.

She would rather leave the life of luxury to which she was accustomed than submit to the odious American merchant who was taking her away from her sister and everything she held dear. She may never have that back, but at least she could ensure her sister was safe.

"I am coming to you, Amelia," she whispered.

The man showed Meg into the small, sparse cottage, which looked to be no more than two rooms. A small kitchen with a table was at one end, and two rocking chairs flanked the stone hearth at the other. A plump matron hurried into the room through a door leading from the kitchen and after a brief explanation from her husband, began to fuss over her visitor.

"So this is what the dogs were barking about. I am Mistress Simpson," she said kindly. "Are you lost?"

"Not precisely, ma'am. I am travelling north."

"At this time of night?" She frowned and doubtless saw more than Meg was comfortable with. "You can go no further tonight, miss. You look done fer. Sam, put the lady in our room and I will make up some pallets here fer us."

"Please do not do that, ma'am. I will take the pallet. I am most grateful for your hospitality."

She clucked with her tongue. "It's nothing but what any good Christian would do. I'd want someone to do the same for our girls when they were young."

Sam walked in with a few worn quilts and a pillow, and in no time Meg was left to her bed in front of the fire. She would not have thought she could sleep in such a way, but she was so very tired. Her hand clutched the handkerchief she had forgotten to leave behind, the one small token she held from her handsome rescuer. Unfurling it, she fingered the beautifully monogrammed "W," hoping her saviour was well.

She fell asleep listening to the dull ticking of an old carriage clock on the shelf above the fire and heard nothing more until woken by the sounds of Mistress Simpson preparing breakfast and the smell of bread baking.

"Good morning, miss. Sorry to wake you, but you best be breaking your fast. My Samuel needs to be off soon."

"Yes, of course." Meg rose and folded the blankets into a neat bundle. Having wrapped her tangled plait into a knot, she tried to brush the wrinkles from her ruined gown. It was hopeless. The mistress set a bowl of porridge before her and worried over her in the same way her old nurse had done.

"I know it is none of my business, miss, but I cannot like you going off alone. It would be clear to a widgeon you are a fine lady."

Meg had to laugh at this pronouncement. Her only gown was ruined from the filthy Channel water, while her hair stank and was hopelessly tangled.

"No longer, I am afraid."

"Did someone take advantage of you? I can see someone at least tried to hurt you."

Meg's hand flew to the bruise she knew marked her face; she could feel others elsewhere. The soldier had almost been too late. A few more moments...

"It is of no matter, now. I must go to my sister."

"I wish me and Sam could do more."

"You have been very kind, ma'am."

"You have a place to go?"

Meg could not lie to this woman, she would see straight through it. "I do not, but I hope to find a position near my sister. We were separated by very bad circumstances."

"Do you know where your sister is?"

Meg shook her head. "Only that his family seat is near Oxford."

"That is far away indeed." She whistled low and kept working.

Grateful for the food, Meg finished her porridge and tidied herself as best she could in the circumstances. As she went out to the cart where Mr. Simpson was loading his goods for market, Mrs. Simpson came to her with a small basket of food.

"My Samuel will take you to my sister in Basingstoke. Mayhap she can arrange for you to travel further with someone safe."

"Oh, Mrs. Simpson! I cannot accept this."

"And I cannot accept you going off on your own. I'll hear no more of it."

Meg gave her a swift hug. "I will never forget you, ma'am. Thank you for keeping my secret." She dropped a graceful curtsy to the goodwife as she would any lady, causing Mrs. Simpson to blush. She smiled and pulling her hood low, climbed into the cart, hoping people would only see what they expected to see.

Riding in a cart was slow and tedious, even more so than a carriage. However, Meg was extremely grateful, for she needed to conserve the few coins she had.

It took two long days to reach Basingstoke, stopping at Petersfield en route to deliver some of the goods. They slept in the barn of one of Mr. Simpson's patrons, where Meg was thankful to be given her own stall. Hoping she had not displaced anyone, she nestled down on some sweet-smelling hay with the blanket provided. It was not what she was used to, but again she was tired enough to sleep. A tabby cat joined her at some point during the night and was snuggled at her feet when she woke.

She had a great deal of time to think during the long days of riding in the cart, as Mr. Simpson was not prone to excessive conversation (which suited Meg very well). It was hard to hide her worry, but at least she had a short reprieve. For one thing, her looks were very distinguishable. If only she had mousy hair and plain eyes! Besides concerns about being recognized, it could cause trouble for her sister.

"You mentioned the stage can be caught from Basingstoke, sir?" she asked, almost thinking out loud.

"Yes, miss. The missus' sister runs the Maidenhead posting house and the stage goes through there twice a week."

She nodded, her thoughts in a whirl, wondering if she might have enough coins for a ticket on the stage and perhaps another dress. She would need to find an employment agency to help her secure a position. References! Raised to run a grand house, she knew that without experience she must have someone to vouch for her. She could forge such a thing if only she had pen and paper.

Things she had once taken for granted must now be considered very dear to a slim purse. There was nothing for it, she would have to beg kindness of Mrs. Simpson's sister. Besides having no pen and paper, she also had very few skills which would be attractive to a grand household. The only thing she could probably do without training was be a housekeeper, a position not easy to come by even were she older and less remarkable in appearance. She did not mean that in a conceited way, she mused honestly, but it was part of the reason her parents had kept Amelia and herself so sheltered in Humberside.

Last evening's attack made her realize just how naïve she had been. Her thoughts flashed back to her rescuer, hoping he endured no lasting harm from his brave actions on her behalf. Saying a quick prayer for his swift recovery, she tried not to allow her thoughts to linger on the handsome face and midnight eyes which she had callously left behind.

CHAPTER 2

*L*uke woke the next morning with a pounding headache. He tried to sit up, but he felt a ripping pain in his thigh. He had thought his injuries were improving. Had a piece of shrapnel become dislodged during the night? The army sawbones had said that might happen, he recalled through a confused haze. Was this a new wound, then, and why was he sleeping in his uniform? He did not remember getting into bed. He then recollected that Tobin had given him enough spirits to fell a small horse. He bellowed at his batman like a sergeant drilling raw recruits.

"Where is the girl?"

Tobin came into the room from the adjoining parlour and averted his eyes, which was unusual. "She is gone, Major."

"Where did she go?"

"I do not know."

"You simply let her walk out of the door without ensuring she was all right? For goodness' sake, she had been attacked!"

"'Tis not precisely what occurred, yer Grace."

"Your Grace? What happened, Tobin?" he growled. Nothing good ever happened when Tobin started 'gracing' him.

"She left out tha' window while the sawbones was here."

"The window?" he repeated with disbelief, looking over to the offending piece of architecture. "What time is it?"

"Half past seven o' the mornin'," the batman replied sheepishly.

"Did you look for her?"

"She left a note." Tobin retrieved it from the small dressing table. Luke could not imagine what had possessed the girl to feel she needed to escape from here unless she feared harm from him as well. He blinked away some of the fog as Tobin returned and handed him the note. "Coffee and toast, Tobin."

"Yes, yer Grace." He bowed and walked to the door. Luke called after him. "If you call me that again, you can find yourself a new position."

Tobin turned around with a barely hidden smirk. "I am only prac-tising, *your Grace*." He closed the door before Luke could hurl some-thing at him. Diverted by the letter in his hand, he opened the paper. A fine gold locket fell into his lap.

KIND SIR,

PLEASE FORGIVE *me for leaving in haste, but you appeared to be in better hands than mine. My presence would only cause further trouble. I must also beg your pardon for borrowing some money. Perhaps my locket will fetch part of their worth. I implore you to forget you ever saw me. I owe you my virtue, if not my life. You have my eternal gratitude.*

I HAVE *the honour to remain your obedient servant,*
  Meg

"WHAT THE DEVIL? Who *are* you, Meg?" he wondered aloud, now more intrigued than ever. Perhaps he would have been able to forget her...perhaps not. It had been a brief glimpse he had caught of the face of an angel beneath the hood, yet the image filled his mind. Who was she hiding or running away from? She had been so helpless and afraid. Clearly she was in some kind of trouble to exchange her beautiful locket for whatever coins she had taken. This was worth far more than pocket change and, unless she had stolen it, indicated she was a lady of some means. He tried to recall anything he could of her, but his overriding impression was that she had smelled as though she had been dragged through the river. She had spoken very little. Her cloak had been of a quality material, but he had not seen her gown. Other than eyes so pale they were almost white, and a few pale blonde wisps of hair, he knew nothing of her.

Tobin returned with his coffee and some toast on a tray and placed it next to him on the bed. "There are some men in the tap-room, asking after some lady they say as went missing off their ship last night."

"Did you say anything to them?"

Tobin gave a derisory laugh, clearly offended. "Of course not. I don't like the look o' them."

His batman was more pretentious than Luke could ever pretend to be.

"Do they say who she was?"

"No, but I think she is in trouble," Tobin added. "She must be to climb out of tha' window. Tha's not an easy drop. She did tell everyone she was your sister. Not that they believed her, but will they be a-tellin' these men about her?"

There was a knock on the door. Luke cursed. Tobin opened it and the innkeeper appeared in the gap, looking worried. "I suppose tha' answers tha' question," Tobin muttered, standing back to allow him to enter.

"There's two men who would like to speak with you in the tap-room, sir," the innkeeper said nervously before bowing himself out.

Luke paused in the act of bringing a piece of toast to his mouth, trying to decide on the best approach. He could refuse to speak to the men, of course, but he wanted to know more and determine how much danger his Meg was in. He could delay his return to ducal affairs a few days longer, for he knew he would not be able to rest until he knew she was safe. As far as the rest of the world knew, he was still away at war.

Before he had decided, Luke heard a scuffle outside the door.

"Let me in," someone bellowed.

The innkeeper's protests were ignored as the door burst open. A man rushed in. He was dressed in dark superfine, but his stays creaked and his corpulent stomach was bulging out from beneath his puce waistcoat. Luke assessed him at a glance: new money, that much was clear.

"Mr. Thurgood!" the innkeeper shouted in protest.

"Where is she?" the odious man demanded. The small room was filled with the man's unwelcome presence.

"Do you find charging into a gentleman's private rooms an effective approach in business?" Luke asked in his most repressive voice.

Instead of apologizing with embarrassment, the intruder kept walking towards him. "Where are you hiding her?" he demanded.

"Come no further or this conversation is over." The man stopped. "Of whom do you speak?" Luke asked, acting bored. If only he had an eyeglass to hand, so he might give him a proper set-down. If this was who Meg had run away from, Luke could not blame her in the least. However, if they were married, this man had the right to enforce her return. The thought made Luke's stomach sour. She had claimed to be a maiden still. Perhaps this man was abducting her for nefarious purposes. He had heard of young girls being sold in the Asian markets.

"My betrothed fell overboard from the *Nancy Jane* and has wandered off."

Luke raised an eyebrow. It normally had the desired effect when he waited for such persons to speak. He suspected she had jumped, in a desperate effort to escape. She was lucky to have survived. It explained a great deal—like her odour, for one.

"Are you quite certain she did not drift out to sea?"

He could see the man waver. Clearly, there was something fishy here, he thought wryly, as the man's eyes darted nervously back and forth.

"I am afraid I have no knowledge of your betrothed, for I was attacked on the street last night and had to be tended by a doctor." He gestured toward his bandage. "I did not leave the room to enjoy any women last night."

The man's face turned purple. Luke knew he should not goad the villain so, but the thought of him with his Meg made his tongue devilish.

"My betrothed is not a strumpet! I will have you know she comes from one of the best families in England!"

"And which family would that be? We might be acquainted. In fact, I could make some enquiries."

The man narrowed his eyes, not that it made a deal of difference. They were already beady and he squinted; it was an unfortunate combination.

"But they said as there was a woman with you, claiming to be your sister!"

"Ah, now I see the misunderstanding. My batman, here, had thought I might be interested in a woman, but when he found I was injured, he sent her away."

"Is yer betrothed dark and voluptuous?" Tobin held his hands out to almost twice the size of his angel.

"No, no. She is the fairest in the land, with eyes like ice and hair like snow." The man almost salivated and Luke swore the rogue would never touch his Meg. The man was still angry, but he would get nowhere with Luke.

"If you happen to find her, send word to my man at the docks. If you would be so kind," he added tritely with a false smile, handing his card to Tobin.

"Bad cess to ye," Tobin muttered just loud enough for Luke to hear as the man departed.

Luke inclined his head but still did not rise. He could be commanding from a sitting position and it was a deliberate snub. He did not care what Mr. Thurgood thought. When the pretentious man had left, which he did by slamming every door possible, Luke rose with purpose, ignoring his wounds.

This action drew a look from Tobin. "Where are ye goin', Major? The doctor said ye needed to stay in bed a week."

Luke cast his frostiest glare upon him. Tobin was unmoved. "You would never have said such a thing to me on the Peninsula. I will not become a wastrel fop simply because we have arrived back in England and you think my title deserving of the same. Mr. Up-To-No-Good means that poor girl harm and I intend to see that does not happen."

MEG HAD NEVER BEEN SO sore in her life. She had felt saddle sore before, of course, but nothing compared to the bumps and bruises she had obtained from two long days in the cart. She breathed a huge sigh of relief when they pulled into the posting house in Basingstoke.

"Let me look to the horses and talk to the Mistress," said Mr. Simpson. Meg climbed down from the cart to survey her surroundings, while holding her hood down tight. She had never been to such a place before. It was crowded and busy and no one paid her any mind, which was more than she could have hoped for. She kept her head low and stood near the wall, for she wanted it to stay that way.

Carriages flew by at a spanking pace, and dust flew up in their wake. Ostlers rushed around with fresh horses for other conveyances and villagers moved purposely about their business. Mr. Simpson returned and escorted her inside through a back door.

"This, here, is the girl I told ye about," he announced, leading her into an enormous kitchen. Glancing up from the roast chicken she was tending, the mistress looked Meg over with a more appraising eye then her sister had. Wearing a lace cap and apron, she nodded, acknowledging their presence.

"Get on with ye then, Sam. I will see her on her way."

"I thank you again for your kindnesses, Mr. Simpson. I will not forget them," Meg murmured, offering her hand.

He blushed a little under her praise and for an instant lightly clasped her fingers. "Just doing my Christian duty, miss. Take care of yerself."

The mistress handed him a basket of food and he left the same way they had come in. Meg desperately hoped he was not the last friend she would find on her journey.

"I am Mrs. Martin. What is your plan, miss?"

"I was hoping to go to London to seek a suitable position."

The woman was plump, like her sister, but she was much sharper. "Have you any experience?" she asked doubtfully.

Meg tried to keep her perfectly manicured, lady's hands hidden in her cloak. "I have been taught to manage a house." It was not precisely a lie but a gross stretch of the truth.

"Have you references?"

"I left rather unexpectedly, but I could make some," she said, hoping she would not offend the woman. Instead, Mrs. Martin cackled her appreciation.

"I would be grateful to work for you to learn more," Meg said earnestly. "It would teach me some necessary skills and I could earn my keep until I can find something."

The woman looked thoughtful. "I cannot have such a one as you in the tap-room. It would cause nothing but trouble."

Meg had no notion of what the woman meant, but did not want to be troublesome. "Perhaps I had better be on my way to London, then. I do not want to cause distress."

"Mayhap with some disguise we could keep you safe."

Safe? Suddenly Meg remembered herself and thought better of it. "I do not wish to be near people." She lowered her head. "I am afraid I had to leave a very bad situation and the man might come looking for me."

"Sam mentioned as much." Mrs. Martin looked her 'guest' up and down and shook her head. Crossing a hallway, she peeped in another door, which, by the sound of it, led to the public rooms. "I will be back in a while. Mind the bar, Sally. Come with me, then, miss." Meg followed the woman up some narrow stairs above the kitchens. One long hallway held numerous doors, presumably to rooms for travellers. Passing these, they went behind a plain door to what Meg assumed was the matron's living quarters. Inside, she could see a sitting room and two other doors, perhaps to bedrooms. The woman went into one and came back with some clothing.

"First, we'll find you a dress and a cap. I am worried about your eyes." Mrs. Martin sorted through the items in her hand, discarding some and choosing others.

Meg was concerned on that count as well. She removed the hood and began to unbutton her cloak. She felt very exposed with her greatest layer of protection gone.

"Lawks, miss! No wonder you're in trouble! No one in their right mind is going to want to hire one as pretty as you. Excepting for a parlour maid or lady's maid, mayhap," she exclaimed, eyeing her critically.

"I cannot be in a house like that! He will surely find me!" Meg wilted and began to cry. They were the first real tears she had allowed herself to shed. So much had happened since her parents' deaths, she had had to be brave and now she did not know if she could continue. What was to become of her?

"There, there, dearie." Warm arms came around her in a gesture of comfort. Meg could not remember the last time she had been held in such a fashion.

When the well was finally dry, she inhaled raggedly and Mrs. Martin stepped back, still holding her though her tone had softened. "We will make do, don't you worry. I will not let the bad man get you. There are some agencies not too far from here, and I can ask about positions. The problem is, with your looks, there are some masters as will feel it their right to take advantage. You are not made for the likes of the tap-room, either. Not that you wouldn't make a pretty penny here, but that is no life for a lady. You are a lady, aren't you?"

Meg gave a slight nod. "That life is lost to me, now. I cannot go back. My uncle virtually sold my sister and I to men who were willing to pay the most, in my case, and offer the highest connection in my sister's. I hope she at least may be comfortable in her situation. I was hoping to find a position near to her so we might have some contact with each other, even if it cannot be openly."

"In Oxford?"

"I know his family estate is there, though I know little else. My uncle was very secretive about the arrangements until the last moment. He knew I would object."

"Turn around, then." The woman began to unfasten Meg's gown, which was ruined. "We will see what we can do with this dress. It would be a pity to waste it. You might have need of it one day."

Meg could not allow herself to hope. Slipping out of her lavender muslin, she donned the garment passed to her by her benefactress–a drab, grey sack of coarse woollen cloth, a white apron and a mob-cap.

Mrs. Martin looked her over with approval. "I'm not sure I would have recognized ye, but we need to do something about those eyes."

"I can look down."

"That will have to do unless we can find some spectacles. For now I will teach you how to do the linens, china and menus. You can learn my duties and that will be a good start while we search for a position. I know of a reputable agency we sometimes hire help from. Most of my help is local during the day. They stay longer that way," she remarked as they walked down the stairs and out behind the stables. "Now, avoid the stable-yard at all costs. That is the busiest place and where most of the men are. We do the laundry inside this wash-house, out here..." She pointed to a large tub within a long, flagged building. "...and then we hang it out to dry on the line in the walled garden. We wash the linens in between every customer," she instructed, adding proudly, "That's why the gents prefer to stop here above the other inns."

Meg just nodded, thinking she had no desire to be anywhere near where she might be recognized.

"We keep fine china only for the highest visitors." Meg followed Mrs. Martin as she returned to the inn and walked into another room, where locked cupboards lined the walls. "If you are in a very fine house, the butler minds the silver and the spirits, and the housekeeper sees to the dishes and the food. I do everything here since we don't tend to serve large gatherings. Sometimes we have a local wedding breakfast..." The woman prattled on. Meg knew all of this and half listened as her mind wandered away to consider bigger problems.

CHAPTER 3

*W*here could she have gone, Tobin?"

"I would suspect London. It is where I would go if I wanted t' hide."

Luke frowned. "She would be swallowed alive by London."

"Aye, depending on who found her. If she found a protector..." He let his voice trail off.

Luke scowled at his man. "Let us hope it has not come to that," he said irascibly, although he had no doubt men would vie for her attention. He prayed he could find her fast, especially if she fell into the wrong hands in London—as she had on the night he rescued her. Why had she not stayed and let him help her? If she was running from that odious merchant, she would probably try to go as far as possible.

"I would not go to London if I were her. I think I would look for a small country village. She cannot last long in Town on the few guineas she has."

"True enough, if that is all she has, but she would find it harder to hide in a small place."

"Either way, she most likely went north from here. We should see if we can follow her trail. However, we must be careful, for Thurgood will also have men searching for her."

Tobin shook his head. "I think you should let it be, yer Grace. If she is mixed up with a man like that, no good can come of it."

"Clearly she did not wish to be. If she has no one else to help her, I cannot leave her to her fate without at least trying. I will send a note to Mr. Graham to make enquiries." His secretary was efficient and discreet, and Luke paid him handsomely for it.

"What are ye goin' to do with her if ye find her?" Tobin asked with impertinence.

"That is none of your concern," Luke snapped.

"Maybe not, but ye are not thinking with yer head. *'Beauty breaks through and pricks them all at last.'*"

"Misquoting Shakespeare again, Tobin? I scarcely saw her face. It is my duty as a gentleman to come to her aid."

"If ye say so, bard."

"Arrange for horses while I write to Graham."

"The sawbones said..." Tobin protested, but knew to stop when Luke held up his hand.

"See to the horses."

Tobin grumbled his way out of the room and Luke laughed. He could not wait to see how his unconventional batman associated with the *ton* servants. It was a good thing he was a duke. Folding the letter and sealing it with wax and his signet ring, he felt confident that they would find her. Graham was a prize amongst secretaries and if Thurgood was looking for Meg, her absence would not be secret for long. Time was of the essence. Within the half-hour, Luke and Tobin were mounted and on their way northward. It was the path he would have taken himself if he had climbed out of the window in the dark.

"How do ye mean to go about this, Major?" Tobin asked, the tone of his voice hinting at his injuries.

"As in stopping at every single cottage and inn along the way, you mean?"

"She did not leave with anyone from the George Inn and she didn't take or steal any o' the horses," Tobin admitted.

"You mean you have already asked downstairs? Tobin, you do have a heart!"

"Don' get used to it," he grumbled. "I can't have you injuring yourself further for some troublesome female."

Luke caught himself before he chastised his batman for speaking ill of the lady. He had to stop being so defensive. Why was he searching so hard? It was not as though she could be his Duchess. He had never thought of his future Duchess as anything other than some enigma he would think of far in the future. That the thought even entered his mind was equally intriguing and disturbing—especially since he knew nothing about her, though he suspected a great deal. Still, it was a dangerous place his mind was going, as if he had little control over his path. He had never really thought he believed in Fate, but were there forces driving him and his actions over which he had little control?

"What's got ye frowning, Major? I'm not sure I like what you're thinking."

"How do you know what I am thinking?"

"To begin with, ye about got yerself killed brawling over a woman. Secondly, we are now planning to chase her across the kingdom. Thirdly, you are a blimey duke, if ye have forgotten, and she don't seem the sort to be a mistress." He ticked off his list on his fingers.

Luke did not agree with taking a mistress. It was part of the reason he had not considered marriage. He wanted to like his wife, hopefully love her. Tobin knew that.

"As I explained before, she needs help and did not appear to have anyone to assist her. I would only hope someone would do as much for my sister were she in need."

"*Mar dhea,*" Tobin muttered to himself in Gaelic, as he was wont to do when he disagreed or was exasperated with Luke, but then said nothing more for a while as they walked their horses, looking for any sign of Meg. Luke had learned not to ask for translations.

"Ye do realize we are not on the London Road?"

"Yes, but would she have realized that in the dark? Something tells me she would have followed the road north from the inn instead."

"I don't know what she would have realized, being tha' we know nothing about her," he retorted.

"I am going to cut out that sharp Irish tongue of yours, one of these days, Tobin."

"Ye've been saying tha' for years... *sir.*"

"One day I might do it, too."

Tobin laughed. He knew the threat was idle, of course. Luke would be dead or rotting in a French prison, were it not for Tobin. The least he could do was put up with his caustic tongue. If he were being honest, he loved bantering with him. Everyone else toadied up to him except for his six—now five—brothers in arms.

"There is a farmhouse off the road, o'er there. Do ye want me to stop an' ask?"

"Yes. We have done nothing else. How far could she have gone on foot?"

"I've no idea. If she had those useless ladies' slippers on and wasn't used t' walkin', then not very far."

They walked the horses up to a gate directly in front of the house. It was small, but tidy.

"Be sweet, Tobin," Luke called as his batman dismounted and tied his reins over a post.

He flashed him a grin and a mocking bow. "Always, yer Grace."

Luke watched as his man knocked on the door, but there was no answer. Luke knew that they could do this for days without finding her. She could have gone in any direction and Thurgood could have many more men out looking. He had started sooner...or, God forbid, she could by lying dead on the side of the road.

"Can I 'elp you?" Luke looked down to see a plump matron wearing a large, floppy white bonnet and holding a basket of eggs. She looked up at him suspiciously.

"Madam, I am looking for a lost young lady, whom I fear may be in trouble."

"What is she to you?"

Luke had to keep his face impassive. He was not used to being spoken to in such a way. If he made her angry, however, she would not tell him anything. He could see Tobin walking back toward them and he would ring a peal over her if he heard her speak thus.

Luke had to think of a good story to give, but he did not know if anyone would believe him, especially if he came after Thurgood. Hopefully the truth would win out.

"She is a friend in trouble. A blackguard came looking for her earlier and alerted us to his intentions."

That must have been the right thing to say, for her face changed from suspicion to caution.

"Aye. I know who you speak of. He was a nasty man and was here not a half-hour 'afore you."

"I hope you did not help him to find her?"

"Lawks, of course I didn't! I wouldn't no more help him even if he offered me a fat purse and proved he was her husband. Anyone could see he'd hurt her."

"Can you tell me where she went? I only want to see her safe."

"And how does I know I can trust you with her? She's a beauty, to be sure. Enough to tempt any warm-blooded male."

Devil take it. He could see Tobin was becoming offended, but he had experience enough with women like this. She could be softened. He decided to come down from atop his high horse, literally. The dappled grey side-stepped as Luke slid down, wincing with pain.

"Please, miss. I am afraid for her on her own."

She liked being called Miss, and he could see her wavering. "Well she ain't precisely alone. My Samuel took her as far as my sister, and I ain't going to say more than that. I promised her."

"If Mr. Thurgood gets to her before I do, there is no telling what he will do to her. You have my word as a gentleman. I mean her no harm."

She frowned. They both knew there were 'gentlemen' who were nothing of the sort. He did not want to use his title, but it seemed Tobin had no such scruples.

"Would ye take his word as a duke?"

He hoped Tobin could feel his disapproving glare.

She narrowed her eyes at him. "You don't look like no duke."

He laughed then. "You are correct. I just arrived in England from serving with the army."

He pulled his signet ring off and handed it to her.

"By George!" She dropped into a curtsy so deep her knee was on the ground.

He extended his hand to help her up and she blushed.

"You promise you will do well by her?"

"I do. I mean to see her restored to her family."

She chewed her lower lip, clearly warring with breaking her word and the girl's safety. "Maybe don't tell her I told you?" She threw up her hands. "Very well, my Samuel gave her a ride to my sister's posting house in Basingstoke. The Maidenhead. It's just off the west London Road."

Luke nodded. "I know the one. It is a fine place." He placed a guinea in her hand and bowed regally. "You have my eternal thanks, madam." He mounted his horse again, refusing to show the woman how much it cost him. She wanted a duke, and he would do nothing to mar that image.

She preened a little. "For what it's worth, I told the other man she went to Bristol."

Luke laughed and winked at her. "You are a jewel among women! If you were not already spoken for, I would be very tempted."

She grinned from ear to ear as he urged his horse forward.

Still, he did not like the thought of Meg being at the mercy of strangers one bit. She must be desperate indeed if she ran away alone. He was more determined than ever to find her... but what would he do when he did?

MEG LOOKED DOWN at her hands, which were raw from the lye soap. How did people do this every day? Did hands become accustomed to the pain? It had been less than one day, and Meg felt as though she had done more work than she had in the rest of her life combined. She vowed if she ever had servants again, she would see that they were compensated handsomely. In one day, she had helped prepare food—

well, she had actually only formed dough into rolls, but it was more than she had ever done before; she had stripped the used beds of their sheets, washed them and hung them out to dry, and now she was finally able to sit down with a basket of mending. That at least she thought she could do. Ladies were taught to use needles from a very young age. She had never done anything more than embroidery, but how different could it be?

"Miss Meg?" Mrs. Martin came in to her private sitting room and sat in the worn floral-patterned chair opposite with a sigh of relief. "It does feel good to get off your feet."

"I do not know how you do it all day," Meg murmured in sympathy.

"You get used to it," she said, her nature pragmatic. "Not but what I don't appreciate a brief rest now and then. I had word back from the agency I use. They have a housekeeper position at some lord's smaller property in Abingdon, near Oxford. It sounded like it was not a residence he frequents, so I could not say if he lets it out or not. They were right impressed with your references, though," she added with a mischievous grin and they both laughed. "I just wished I knew more about the situation you'd be going to. If you ever need to come back you are welcome here. I know it's not what you're used to, but you'll be treated fairly."

"Thank you, ma'am. You have been more kind than I could have hoped for."

"Not to your hands," Mrs. Martin added with a whistle when she noticed Meg's red, raw appendages.

"As you say, ma'am, I will grow accustomed to it."

"Let us pack your gown. With new trimmings, it can be made presentable. I'll be sending you by cart in the morning, with Georgy, who will take you to the agency in London."

"Why do I go to London?" Meg asked doubtfully.

"They will send you on from there," she replied.

"How can I ever repay you?"

"Do not worry about a thing. You have saved me some work this morning." Mrs. Martin answered without looking Meg in the eye, pretending to be busy with folding her lavender day gown.

"Hardly enough to compensate for a ride all the way to London!" Meg protested.

"'Twill be safer than on the stage, miss. No one who has ever seen you could forget you. You can trust my Georgy. He may be a simple man, but he won't harm you, neither, and he is a good driver."

Impulsively, Meg wrapped her arms around the woman, quite likely frightening her to death, but she was just so grateful for Mrs. Martin's and Mrs. Simpson's help. She knew very well what fate could have befallen her. It still could.

"Send word to me once you're settled, just for me peace of mind. I hope you find yourself close to your sister and the monster leaves you alone. Oh! I almost forgot," she said, reaching into her pocket. "Nelly found these in our odds and ends. You would not believe what the swells leave behind." She unfolded her hands to reveal a gold-rimmed pair of spectacles.

Meg placed them on the end of her nose and had to squint to see through them, almost losing her balance.

"I almost didn't recognize you! But you'll do, miss."

"If I am not mistaken for the town drunk," Meg added dryly, wondering how she could manage to perform her duties, let alone see, with these for a disguise.

"You only have to wear them when others are around. If the agency is correct, you won't have many other servants or guests to worry over."

"I pray they are correct."

There was a knock on the door and Bart, the stable-boy, ran breathlessly into the room. "Mistress, some toff is as asking after a lady!"

Meg gasped. How had they found her already?

"He must have the luck of the devil. Go down the backstairs and wait. I'll have Georgy bring the cart around. It's not ideal but there's to be a good moon tonight. I'll tell them you went on to London. They could spend weeks there looking for you."

Only weeks? Hopefully, by then she could find Amelia. If she was found before her birthday, she did not know if she would be able to escape again.

CHAPTER 4

*L*uke was feeling quite the gallant knight by the time they arrived at the posting house. He directed the horse through the entrance with anticipation, feeling happier than he had in years. For a moment, he considered singing like Don Quixote, at the top of his lungs, but somehow thought Tobin might not like the implication he was the companion, Sancho—however mad he might think this quest of chivalry.

"You might want to wipe that moonstruck look off yer face, Major. She might want nothing to do with ye."

"I was just thinking of Don Quixote." It was one of the novels they had read on the long nights sitting around the camp-fire.

Tobin grunted. "Need I remind you tha' he was quite mad? Though ye have not yet attacked any windmills or murdered any sheep."

"I can see you are in no mood for humour today." Ignoring the pains in his leg, which long days in the saddle did nothing helpful for, he slid gingerly from the horse. He noticed the hustle and bustle in the stable-yard and frowned. Was his Meg trying to hide in such a busy place?

Tobin was also frowning as a young stable-boy came forward to take their reins.

"Excuse me, lad. We are looking for a lady. Can you show me to your mistress, so I may ask about her?" He tossed a shilling to the boy, whose eyes were wide with awe and he bobbed his head up and down before running away to do the errand. If anything, more of a racket ensued. A donkey cart careered through the yard as if on a mission for the Crown and Luke shook his head in dismay.

"D'ye want me to speak to the proprietor?" Tobin asked.

"I can manage." Luke walked into the tap-room to request refreshment while Tobin took care of the horses. He certainly hoped Meg was here because he was exhausted. A plump matron hurried down the stairs towards him, panting heavily. She was the spitting image of the woman from the farm. He was glad Tobin was not there, for you could always catch more flies with honey than vinegar. He put on his (hopefully) most charming smile and gave her a deep bow.

"How can I help you, my lord?"

She was guessing as to his status and was not far off. He would not enlighten her unless necessary.

"I would like to remain discreet."

She nodded and ushered him into a private parlour seemingly reserved for travelling gentry. It looked much like any other he had encountered across the breadth of England with panelled walls, a dining table with chairs and a stone hearth.

"Well? Bart says you were asking after a lady?"

Luke had already decided to be as honest as possible. It had worked well for the sister.

"I am looking for a lady, who is being chased by a blackguard claiming to be her betrothed."

"What kind of lady?" She scowled at him.

"A respectable one who is in a great deal of trouble, madam. I only want to help her before Thurgood gets his hands on her. She ran away because she was afraid and has little money. You must not have seen her or you would know. She has the face of an angel, with white hair and ice-blue eyes."

"She was here."

"Was?"

35

She nodded her head. "The day before yesterday. She happened to catch the London stage in good time."

"London?" Luke swallowed.

"She said something about finding a position."

"A position?" She must think him inarticulate, but he had held high hopes for finding Meg here. "Forgive me, I am disappointed. I cannot begin to imagine what trouble might befall her in London. Thank you for your assistance." He pulled out his card and handed it to her. "If you happen to see her again or hear word, you may reach me here."

She did not even look at the card. She was gnawing her lower lip in the same way her sister had.

"If a Mr. Thurgood comes looking for her, please send him in the wrong direction." He placed two gold coins in her hand and walked out of the parlour, feeling dejected. Tobin was waiting in the tap-room for him, enjoying a pint of ale.

"Do not grow too comfortable. She went to London."

"*Imeacht gan teacht ort,*" Tobin muttered.

Luke could sympathize. He had to go to London anyway, so he might as well do it now rather than later.

After a quick pint of ale and simple meal of stew, he reluctantly headed for the carriage Tobin had ordered. He did not even protest, grateful to be off the horse.

MEG RUSHED DOWN the backstairs and waited inside the door for Georgy to bring the cart up. She heard a few drops of rain start to fall and instantly thought of the sheets she had left out to dry. How quickly her perspective in life had changed! Never before had she given thought to the linens. She dare not risk anyone seeing her now if she attempted to go and pull them from the line, especially if there was someone here asking for her. It had to be Mr. Thurgood, for who else would care? Her uncle could not yet know of her escape.

Waiting was hard! Surely a quick peek would be all right? She opened the door a crack. A whiff of air met her, pungent from exerted horses and their leavings, except she could see nothing apart from the cobbled yard. Craning her head around the door, hoping to see what was going on, she saw Georgy's face.

"I'm bringing the cart, miss and you can climb in. Best not to be seen, me mam said."

"Yes, Georgy," she replied sweetly and shut the door.

It was agony waiting, not knowing if she would fall back into the claws of that awful man. For who would help her now? Her heart beat so loudly that she could scarcely determine what was happening on the outside. She looked again, and saw the monster's face speaking to one of the grooms. She jumped back inside. He had found her! An involuntary cry escaped her. She had been so careful! Was she never to be rid of him? Would he track her down no matter where she hid? Was there anywhere safe? It was hard to imagine he sought her for anything more than damaged pride. Regardless of how much he had paid her uncle for her hand, Thurgood was rumoured to be rich as a nabob.

She felt utterly sick. There was nothing she did not think she would do to avoid that man. When she thought of his rotten teeth and his lecherous eyes…she fought back the contents of her stomach as they threatened to reappear. At last, she heard hooves and wheels before the door. Pulling her hood as low as she could to hide herself and shelter from the rain, she opened the door of the carriage that was pulled neatly in front of the back entrance. "How thoughtful of Georgy," she muttered. Perhaps he did not know the difference between a cart and a carriage. As she put her foot on the first step, however, she heard the unmistakable voice.

"That carriage! Has anyone searched that carriage?" he bellowed.

A voice behind her said, "Get inside quick, miss. Under the seat."

She did as she was told, praying that was Georgy giving her instructions. Whomever they were seemed to wish her away from Thurgood, at any rate.

Grateful to be a small person, it was still a tight fit under the seat. Thankfully, her nose was near a small area of fretwork; if she could only be calm she could survive. She had never liked small spaces.

The door to the carriage was thrust open, and Meg was certain she would be discovered, for her heart sounded like drums pounding and her breath seemed as loud as a gale.

"I beg your pardon... Thurgood, was it not? You seem to have mistaken the carriage. This one is mine," a familiar voice said with hauteur.

"You again! I do not suppose you have seen the girl?" The rough tones carried the unmistakable accent of the shop.

"Ah, yes. I forgot you had misplaced your betrothed. I have not had the privilege. Now, if you will excuse me, I must be on my way. Tobin!" The man called to his servant and climbed inside.

Meg's mind was searching furiously to comprehend. Was this the man who had saved her the first time? Was he saving her again? She knew she should feel relief, but her heart sank. This was not her plan! Had she mistaken the carriage? Where was this one headed? She needed to find Amelia. Someone shouted to spring the horses and the carriage lurched forward. It was so very cramped and warm inside this little box. It smelled of wet blankets and old boots. However, she was too afraid to try to escape. She dare not conjecture what her fate would be with this man, either, although she suspected nothing could be worse than Thurgood. She closed her eyes and tried to settle her breathing so the man inside would not suspect her presence. She would just have to stay where she was until the next stop. Hopefully, whoever had ordered her inside would help her then.

Once the carriage seemed to steady on the highway, she dared open her eyes. The fretwork was small, and it was dark inside, but she could just make out the face of her saviour sitting on the opposite bench. His long legs were outstretched and relaxed as he looked out of the window. She took the opportunity to stare unashamedly at his handsome face. There had been no time to study his features before, when she was doing her best to hide her own from recognition. His strong, unshaven jaw, dark locks and blue eyes were the stuff of a damsel's dreams... and it was not long before the fatigue of work, combined with suffocating heat and swaying movement, duly lulled her to sleep.

Meg jerked awake. She tried to move her arms but was met by resistance on both sides. Her legs were curled up almost to her chest and she began to panic. A scream would have been welcome if she could have managed it. She could not think coherently and tears began to roll down her face. To her relief, at the same moment, the lid to this coffin was lifted.

"Are ye all right, miss? I did not expect ye to stay in there the whole time." She concentrated on his Irish drawl.

"I did not know whose carriage I was in. Should I have emerged like a genie from a bottle?" she asked testily.

His green eyes twinkled at her outburst, but the rest of him was stern. This was definitely the soldier's man from Portsmouth.

"Ye should not have run away before. My master has been lookin' for ye. He wants t' help."

"Why would he want to trouble with me?"

"Actin' the maggot, is what." The man muttered his opinion. "He has a misplaced, gentlemanly notion of chivalry."

"But I do not want to be found."

"I suspected as much but he would hear none o' it. What do ye want me t' do, then? He will be back in a moment."

She pondered her options, not that she had many. "Where are you going?"

"To London. The proprietress told him ye had taken the stage there."

Meg could not help but offer a grateful smile. But still, they had both found her!

"I can try to help ye better from London. Ye will be taking a great risk, gettin' out here. Ye have been fortunate in yer friends thus far."

"Yes I have," she said softly. "Very well, I will suffer this box to London."

Her face must have shown her reluctance.

"I could give ye my spot on top with Georgy and ride with the master."

"You do not think he would notice?"

"We will make sure he doesn't. Quick, come with me."

39

"Thank you, sir." She was truly grateful for his kindness, especially when she was able to stand in the fresh air on her own two feet.

"Don't thank me, thank me master."

"If you say so," she remarked with scepticism. True to his word, he helped her hide behind the carriage until the soldier was ensconced inside. Then he lifted her up to the box next to Georgy, who smiled with pleasure at her. He gave Georgy directions as to where to let her off in London, and he would find her there. She had never ridden on the outside of a carriage before and it was a liberating experience. It smelled earthy and fresh from the recent rain. She even lifted her face to the sun for a few moments as they rolled through the open countryside. It would be necessary to return to hiding soon, but she was grateful for the short reprieve.

CHAPTER 5

*T*obin was acting strangely. He never rode inside a close conveyance, always saying it made him claustrophobic. Luke eyed him dubiously.

"Riding inside, Tobin? To what do I owe the rare honour?"

"I don' like the look o' the clouds."

"You are in England. They always look suspect. However..." Luke lifted the screen to peer at the blue, almost cloudless sky. "I think you are safe for a while." He raised an eyebrow and crossed his arms, waiting for his man to answer.

"No need to be high and mighty with me. There wasn't room. Georgy is giving a lad a lift to London."

That was not an unheard-of thing to do. Luke sighed. "I am surprised he convinced you to give up your seat."

"I have endured worse."

"I should say so," Luke retorted, beginning to feel amused.

"It is not so far now. What do ye mean to do next?"

"I suppose I shall have to return to my duties."

"Ye are giving up on the girl?"

"Graham is making enquiries. I suppose I shall have to be content with that."

Tobin grunted. He was prone to doing that when he should be holding his tongue.

"You might as well say whatever it is you are thinking. I am aware you do not approve of my trying to help the poor girl."

"I can't say as I don' feel a mite sorry for her," Tobin admitted. "But ye are a Duke and cannot traipse all over the kingdom in search of someone ye do not even know. She could be an adventuress or that scoundrel's mistress for all we know."

"Somehow, I highly doubt the latter." He doubted the former as well, but knew protesting would fall on deaf ears.

"I have a feeling the girl will be all right. I think the mistress at the posting house took care of her."

"Why do you say that?"

"Because 'dear Georgy' said as much when I convinced him to take us to London."

"Georgy, the driver? Did he say where she was going?"

"No, he did not know. Of that I am convinced. I don't think he is capable of lying."

Luke trusted his man's judgement. It had saved him before, although he could tell he was not telling him the whole story.

"We will have to trust that it is so and hope Graham can trace her."

Tobin crossed himself with a skyward glance and began a conversation with himself in Gaelic. Luke waited until he had ceased.

"Yes?"

"There is no good can come of this, Major."

"If Graham finds her and she is safe, I will let it be. I promise."

Tobin looked doubtful.

"I realize she may be only the beautiful daughter of a merchant, but even if she is a lady, very likely she will be ruined once word gets out."

Tobin nodded. "I am glad ye can see that. I was concerned ye would take some strange fancy into yer head."

"She is uncommonly beautiful."

"She is braw," he agreed. Nevertheless, Luke was aware his batman still watched him warily.

"Sadly, we both know what happens to young, beautiful women without support. And if her story is true, she is in trouble due to no fault of her own."

Tobin did not reply this time, but glared.

"So, naturally, she would be condemned to life on the streets or as a slave to Thurgood."

"Now ye are twistin' my words, Major."

"Merely reasoning through the situation and why I am trying to help," he drawled.

Tobin had closed his eyes, but one popped open to show his disapproval before he closed it again and nodded off. Luke had always envied his batman's ability to sleep anywhere yet remain alert. Tobin was right, though, curse him.

Perhaps it was just he who was not right in the head. He could not let it go, however. Something was compelling him to try to find Meg. Was it those haunted, unforgettable eyes? Were they haunting him?

When they had encountered Thurgood at the posting house, Luke had known the man would never give up until he found Meg. Luke had already subconsciously made the decision to find her first, but he could not allow a man like that to have any woman unwillingly. Would she allow him to help? First, he had to find her.

MEG HOPPED off the box when they reached the back alley to their destination. She walked towards the mews and waited, hood down, hoping no one would notice. Nervously, she fingered the handkerchief that was still in her pocket, hoping Luke, whomever he was, remained as gracious once he found out about her deception.

It felt like an hour before Tobin returned for her, but he did at last. Remarkably, no one seemed to have noticed her.

"I had t' clear the way for ye with the housekeeper," he said—by way of apology, she guessed. "She didn't like it, o' course, but she agreed to let ye help in the kitchen for the time bein', as long as you don't cause no trouble. Then I had to get Cook to agree."

He began leading her towards the house. It was a three-storey, white stone mansion in the newer fashioned Palladian style, complete with Doric columns, Venetian windows and a stone balustrade along the roof-top. It was palatial! Did her family's town house look like this?

"Ye will have a room in the attics, like the rest of the servants." He looked sideways at her as if afraid she would object.

"That will suit me very well." She stood taller in protest in case he was testing her. If he knew where she had slept the past few days, he would not question her sensibilities. "Will I have any time to search for my sister?"

"Yer sister? Is she missing too?"

"Not precisely." She sighed with resignation. "I can be assured of your continued confidence?"

"O' course, but I will only keep it from my master as long as it doesn't risk yer safety."

She began to protest but stopped again almost at once and leaned against the wall before they went inside. "I suppose I can ask no more of you."

"I think ye might need to start from the beginnin'. Much though I don't want to be involved, it seems I am."

"I do apologize. This is not how I envisioned things happening, either."

He grunted strangely and muttered something in another language. Was it Gaelic? The only words she made out were *'gommeril'* and *'sassenach'*. He was an interesting creature. He might even be handsome, with his black hair and green eyes, if he were not perpetually scowling at the world.

"I will be succinct. My parents died in a boating accident a few months ago. My sister and I were left to the guardianship of our uncle. He had always seemed a decent fellow, the few times I had met him, but it was not long until it became apparent that he was not interested in our welfare at all. He sold me to an American merchant, Mr. Thurgood, to the tune of a hundred thousand pounds, and has arranged a marriage for my younger sister to a decrepit old lord. His main estate is in Oxfordshire and that is where I was trying to reach, to see if I could save her before it is too late."

She thought she saw a flash of sympathy in his hard gaze, but it was gone before she could be certain.

"I will reach my majority in three months, so I must remain hidden until then. Amelia, however, is but seventeen and is extremely naïve and trusting."

"Will she go along willingly?"

"I am certain, if she protests, he will threaten her in some manner, just as he did me. I fell asleep in my bed at the Abbey and woke up on a ship with a raging megrim. I was only able to escape the ship by sending the servants away. Thank goodness no one suspected I would jump ship or it would be too late."

"Thurgood drugged ye. He is a right vile scoundrel. May the divil take his last shilling!" he cursed.

"Indeed. Will you help me, Tobin?" she pleaded.

"I'll see what I can do for ye, miss, but I think we should tell the Major. He has his men searchin' for ye. If word gets out yer missin', ye will be ruined in Society."

"I care nothing for that, only that my sister is safe. I considered myself ruined the moment my uncle sold me."

"I won't lie to the Major, but I will do my best to keep yer presence mum. Ye have to do yer part, though."

She nodded and pulled the horrid spectacles from her pocket and put them on, eliciting a chuckle from the batman.

Meg wished she could have seen his face with a smile, but her vision was distorted dreadfully. "It is bad enough without you making fun," she chastised.

"It is a good disguise," he conceded.

"If only I could see," she mused.

Surprisingly, he took her arm and guided her through the back door of the very large mansion. She had not fully appreciated how large it was while standing behind the mews.

"Cook, this is..." He hesitated and she spoke up.

"Meg." *Might as well stick as close to the truth as possible*, she thought grimly.

"She is my cousin from Ireland and the master agreed to let her come here for a while and learn. I appreciate your kindness."

So much for the truth, Meg thought dryly.

"Get on with you then, Tobin. I'll take care of the lass."

He gave her one last glance and then left her alone in a cavernous stone-walled room, warm from the rolling fires cooking large pots on the hob.

"Do you know anything about the kitchen?" The woman looked her up and down and likely found her wanting, before handing her an apron. Meg could only imagine the picture she presented.

"I know how to form rolls."

"Well that's something, then," the cook replied. "Now you can learn how to peel potatoes." She set down a large pot of them in front of her, demonstrated how to do it once and then handed her a knife.

Meg was grateful for the mind-numbing task. It allowed her to forget her troubles for a while as she determined the best way to peel the skin from the flesh. After she had become proficient enough not to waste half the tuber, her mind wandered back to her sister. First, she would need to find a copy of *Debrett's Peerage*, and then she would need to find a way to post a letter. She could only pray Tobin's patience would not run out before she found Amelia.

CHAPTER 6

$\mathcal{L}$uke soon settled into a routine. His teams of stewards and land agents had managed well in his absence, but seemed grateful for him to ease the burden. There were some decisions that had been put off awaiting his return, however, and he threw himself into his duties with equal determination as he had as a soldier. If he worked himself into exhaustion every day, he found it was easier to grasp a few hours' sleep.

Mr. Graham knocked and entered as per their morning ritual. The young secretary, dressed in a neat suit of plain dark cloth, bowed and sat in the chair across from Luke's desk with his prepared reports and correspondence.

"Is there any new word today?" Daily, he asked for reports on Meg, but she seemed to have disappeared from the face of the earth.

Graham knew what he was asking. If he thought his employer was on a wild goose chase, he was kind enough not to say so.

"Our people trailing Thurgood have reported that his men appear to have stationed themselves in Oxfordshire. They had taken up residence at the Old Crown in Faringdon."

"Has there been any sign of her there?"

"Not to my knowledge, your Grace. We have men searching, and men keeping an eye on Thurgood's men."

Luke nodded.

"Thurgood himself has returned to London. He must have realized that heralding her escape about would make him look ridiculous."

"I think you give him too much credit, but let us pray he has come to his senses. Has there been any gossip?"

"Not that I have seen in the papers, your Grace. I am not privy to the tongues of the matrons," he added in the manner of a suggestion, which Luke wanted to ignore.

"I have not seen anything in the news-sheets either, which is good. I suppose I could bestir myself to see if there is gossip." How could she have disappeared into thin air? The thought bothered him, but as long as Thurgood did not have her they were still better off, were they not?

"I still have not received word from the jeweller."

"It is doubtless nothing more than a trinket any young lady would have. Have you looked at the brothels?"

Graham's cheeks coloured at this. His secretary was still a very green youth.

"Yes, your Grace. I have not enquired myself, but my sources tell me no one of that description has recently arrived at the well-known places."

Luke ran one of his hands through his hair. There was little more he could do, and he knew it. Nonetheless, something inside was nagging at him and he could not simply forget about her. Perhaps he was a romantic at heart, and he was as mad as Don Quixote. He could hear Tobin's scathing remarks to that notion.

"Shall I keep looking, your Grace?"

At some point in the discussion, Tobin had slipped into the room. He must be bored, wasting his talents as a valet. Luke would need to think of something more to occupy the man's time.

"Still looking for the girl?" Tobin asked as he slid into the other armchair in front of the desk.

"With very little luck, I am afraid," Graham replied.

"Hopefully it means she has found a safe place to hide." Tobin picked up a paperweight and fingered the bronze-cast bull.

"I cannot be easy until I find her," Luke replied.

"Have ye searched for a family with two sisters? I would swear she said she was lookin' for her sister." Tobin's gaze was overly focused on the paperweight.

"You are just now thinking to mention this?" Luke asked, exasperated.

"How was I to know what ye heard and did not? Ye were much more interested in her than I."

"One of these days, I shall throttle you, Tobin." Luke shook his head. "We are shocking Mr. Graham."

The batman shrugged. "He'll survive."

"I want to know everything you know about her, even if you think it is insignificant. I was rather preoccupied from the brandy you gave me, if you recall."

"Ye do not remember being sewn up, do ye?"

Luke gave his best withering look but Tobin was unaffected.

"Georgy said—" he began.

"Georgy?" Luke interrupted.

"The driver from the posting house," Tobin explained, as if he were daft. Perhaps he was.

"Carry on." He waved his hand.

"Georgy said he was travellin' to London so I convinced him to drive us as well. I assumed yer men had been back to speak with everyone there."

Luke frowned, then looked at his secretary, who nodded. "That is correct, your Grace. It is how we discovered Thurgood's men and followed them from there to Oxford."

"Then it seems to me, if Thurgood's men are there, perhaps the sister is there? Or the girl might be there?" Luke closed his eyes. "If she is there, why have they not found her?"

"Mayhap she is in London," Tobin suggested.

Tobin was acting strangely—again. Did he know something more that he was not telling?

"Or perhaps she duped us like she did Thurgood?"

"Perhaps now you may search for a family with two sisters, Graham?" Tobin suggested.

"My instinct tells me she comes from gentry, if not nobility. There was a presence about her, besides her speech," Luke added.

"Yes, your Grace." Graham bowed and left. Luke was still not used to such formality, but it was clear the secretary would never be as comfortable with barrack-room manners as he and Tobin.

Luke fixed his attention back on his batman. "What are you not telling me?"

"I don't know what ye mean," he answered evasively.

"You are not yourself. What else do you know about the girl? If you know something, you must tell me. It could mean life or death for her."

"I wish I could tell ye more, Major. D'ye want me to ask around?"

"Do you fancy yourself a Runner, now, Tobin? Or do you have some acquaintances here of which I was unaware?"

Tobin straightened himself. Was he taking offence? Luke almost laughed at his expression.

"I happen to have some acquaintances amongst other gentlemen's men. I discovered they haunt Pontack's Tavern."

"Do they? That could be useful, I suppose."

"Who d'ye know with estates near Oxford?" Tobin asked.

Luke laughed. "I cannot think of anyone other than Marlborough. What I would not give to be a fly on the wall while you try to gossip!"

"At least I am trying to help. Why don't ye take yourself off to somewhere and do the same?"

"Insolent wretch." Luke scowled, but knew Tobin was right. He could avoid Society no longer.

MEG KEPT to herself and tried to remain as inconspicuous as possible. It was not too hard to do. It was such a large house, and she was not the only new servant hired with the master's return. She had been desperately waiting for a time when said master would leave so she could do some more searching for her sister. Also, Tobin had been helpful, seeking her out on occasion to enquire how she did and let her know his doings. It had been three days since her arrival and the Major had not once left the house! She had peeled more carrots, kneaded more dough and cracked more eggs than she had ever imagined possible, and most of it was simply to feed the servants! Cook had taken her to market, which was a welcome reprieve from being closeted in the kitchen. Cook was being truly kind and very, very patient with her ignorance.

As she mindlessly kneaded some more dough, a spray of flour went into the air as Tobin entered the kitchen and he waved his arms to see through the cloud of dust. The room was mostly empty at this point, it being late afternoon. They had just sent tea upstairs and were soon to start on supper preparations.

"Tobin, stop harassing my girls and get your rascally self out of my kitchen!" Cook chastised the batman.

He gave her a devilish half smile and plucked a remaining jam tart from the table and popped it in his mouth. He closed his eyes and moaned a noise of appreciation, making a great scene out of it. Nothing was surer to mollify Cook, by the look she gave him.

Her hands were on her hips, but her face beamed. "What do you want, then? Did I not send you enough for tea so you thought to come and pilfer mine and Meg's?"

"Is it possible to have too many of yer jam tarts?"

She snapped his knuckles with a towel. "Stop bamming me, you rogue. It might work on the maids, but just say what you want and get on with it. I have dinner to prepare!"

Meg thought the tactic was working very well, and knew if Tobin applied himself to being this charming very often, he could be quite dangerous.

"I've come to escort Miss Meg to the library," he said quietly. "His Grace has gone to call on Lady Crewe."

Meg looked up hopefully at Cook, who nodded and made a shooing motion. Tobin had already crept away and was waiting on the other side of the door. It would not do for them to be seen leaving together, not that anyone was there to watch at the moment.

Standing in the shadows ahead of her, she followed discreetly through the narrow, servant's corridors until he stopped and opened one of the doors. She followed him into the library, a beautiful two-storey, golden-hued room with books from floor to ceiling on two sides, a wall of windows on the third, and the fourth was the door through which the family would enter, the portal surrounded by landscapes.

She stopped. Her saviour was a duke? Tobin had very distinctly said 'his Grace' in the kitchen! Moving slowly forward again, she knew it was even more imperative that she find her sister and leave here as quickly as possible, for she did not want to soil her saviour's good name. It also explained why he felt he had the right to interfere.

The way her life had changed in less than a week was still unreal to her. It would be easier to fall into despair, but that would not save Amelia. Tobin stopped at one of several tables and pointed to a large, leather-bound book.

"Here is the *Debrett's Peerage* you were asking after. Ye should have seen the look on Mr. Graham's face when I asked for it." There was that devilish half-smile again.

"I appreciate your help more than you know, Tobin."

She removed her glasses, rubbing the bridge of her nose. They caused horrible headaches and she removed them whenever she could. He already knew she was a fraud. She sat down at the table where the book lay, feeling great pleasure in removing her weight from her feet.

"Have you remembered anything else? I overheard Mr. Graham telling the Major that Thurgood had men near Oxford, but he himself had remained in London."

Meg looked up with surprise.

"It would help greatly if I could tell them who ye are," he suggested.

"No! I do not want him involved."

"It is too late for that, miss. It won't be long before he discovers who ye are. He still doesn't know ye are here, however. I wish ye would let me tell him. 'Twould save a lot of trouble."

Meg did not like this one bit. She felt deeply conflicted, but she had not asked the Duke for help and he could make things worse for Amelia. She no longer cared for her own reputation.

"Can you not persuade him otherwise?"

Tobin let out a harsh laugh. "Ye do not understand the Major at all. He has a very strong sense of chivalry and feels it is his duty as a gentleman to help ye." Then, as if it needed more explanation, he added, "He has a sister, himself."

Meg dropped her head into her hands. "This is a disaster! I must find my sister quickly and end this charade!"

"'Twould be o'er much quicker if we knew who ye were. I will not tell him outright without yer permission, I gave ye my word. Nevertheless, he does know ye have a sister and he has gone out to see if there's been any gossip."

Things were far worse than she knew. She felt like she would retch. "I do not know what is best to do, Tobin."

"He only wants to help."

"If he has an overweening sense of chivalry as you say, when he finds out who I am and that I have been living in his house, what will he feel obligated to do then? No, I cannot do it."

"Will you at least tell me who ye are?"

She hesitated, considering. So far, he had kept his word.

"I cannot see what good it will do, but I am Lady Margaret Blake and my sister is Lady Amelia. She is to wed the Earl of Erskine and I do not know whether it is yet too late to save her. I believe my uncle might wait for mourning to be observed, since Society will question if he does otherwise. It is the only circumstance he restrains himself for."

Tobin stared at her silently for a few minutes, which was more disturbing than if he had been chastising her in Gaelic. She had overheard he was Irish. One day, she would very much like to know how he came to be the Duke's man, but just now she had other, more pressing considerations. With that reminder, she began thumbing through the book about the Peerage.

"Could he not be a duke? There are only two dozen of those," she muttered as she scanned the hundreds of pages listing the heritage of all the nobility in the kingdom.

It was not long before she found what she needed. "The Earl of Erskine's country seat is in Faringdon, Oxfordshire."

"You found the one you need?" Tobin asked from across the room, where he had been looking around a shelf of leather-bound books.

"Yes, but how do we discover if she is there? He could have other estates and quite likely a residence in London. Or she may still be with my uncle."

"I suspect it will be easy enough to discover if he is in Town. Ye leave that to me."

"You can easily find out?"

"I suspect ye could as well. Have ye not discovered how to gossip?" He looked astonished, with his eyes wide and his brows raised.

Meg had not had anyone to gossip with before, and Cook did not approve. She shook her head.

"It seems, Tobin, that I am at your mercy yet again." She did not like feeling beholden. "I do not know if I will ever be able to repay you."

"Don't ye worry about tha'," he said gruffly. "If ye are safe, then my master is happy."

She felt her lips curve into a slight smile. He did not like being praised; that much was clear. She reached over and took his hand.

"Nevertheless, I am still very, very grateful."

CHAPTER 7

*L*uke was more afraid of his godmother than any French soldier. In fact, he would rather face off with Napoleon than her. Every man in Society quaked in her presence, for she had forced more marriages, duels and ruination of character than anyone else in Town. To be fair, most of the people were probably guilty of what she accused them of, but she felt it her duty to intervene. What must it be like, he wondered, to be such a person that everyone did your bidding out of fear of you…did she have any true friends?

He leaned on his cane as he walked the short distance to her house. He wore his new jacket by Weston and new boots by Hoby. It was astonishing how quickly people catered to a duke. It was disgusting, actually.

Tipping his hat to some young ladies walking with their maids, he frowned when a gaggle of feminine giggles followed behind. Somehow, he did not think Meg would titter or giggle. With that thought, he lifted the knocker on number ten, Queen Street and prepared his strategy.

"Good afternoon, your Grace." He was greeted by the butler and could not recall his name. *Cursed memory.* Nodding instead, he walked into the marbled entry hall, which was consumed by a three-storeyed white staircase and walls severed with doors.

"I trust you are well?" he asked the man, whose face remained unflappable. His godmother would demand nothing less, of course. Her consequence gave him consequence.

"Yes, thank you, your Grace. Lady Crewe is receiving in the drawing room this afternoon." The bewigged servant in livery spoke without moving a muscle other than his mouth.

"Are there many callers present?"

"The last gentleman has just left, sir." He glanced at the clock to indicate civilized calling hours were over. That suited Luke perfectly.

"Follow me, your Grace, and I will announce you."

"There is no need," he replied, walking past the man and slowly taking the stairs to the second floor. He paused at the door to take a fortifying breath before knocking.

"Enter," she commanded.

Luke stepped through the door. She did not even look up; she was no doubt expecting a servant.

"Good afternoon, Godmother. You look extremely well." In truth, she had not aged well at all, but it would be grossly unkind to voice such a thing. Her skin was drooping over her jowls, a fine counterpoint to the severity with which her hair was pulled back to each side, making her look more fierce. Perhaps you began to look like your personality when you aged.

"Waverley!" She jumped in her chair and her hand flew to her breast as though an intruder had surprised her.

"Had you not heard I was in Town?" He bowed over her extended hand and kissed the air above it. "I always thought you were privy to everything."

"I had heard rumours," she acknowledged, "but had not seen proof with my own eyes until this very moment." She sniffed indignantly.

"You are my first call," he confided. "I had to wait for proper attire to be made."

Somewhat mollified by this pronouncement, she looked him up

and down with approval. "Now, be seated and stop looking down at me. I am tired of craning my neck."

"I thought you would never ask." He sat as normally as he could in the puce armchair with a lace cloth covering the top which looked identical to the one pinned to her head. He did not wish for her to know the extent of his injuries. Most likely it was no secret to her that he had been sent home for his wounds. "I trust you are well?"

"As well as can be expected for a lady of my age. Did you really come here for polite chit-chat?" Her gaze narrowed with suspicion.

"I came to see my favourite godmother," he said sweetly. "I have been gone over two years. Who better than to apprise me of the necessary happenings of the *ton?*"

"I do not know why you would say that. I am no gossip." She feigned offence, while at the same time looking pleased.

Luke did his best not to appear annoyed. It was a game she liked to play. He flattered, she pretended and eventually she would tell him what he wished to know.

"Deaths? Marriages?" he suggested, tapping his long fingers in a rhythm along the chair's arm.

She placed her pointing finger against her chin, causing the unfortunate jowls to wiggle. Luke looked out of the window momentarily so he would not laugh. It was going to be a tedious afternoon to extract the information he sought.

"Have you already taken tea?" she asked, as any good hostess would. "I do not keep spirits in my house, you will remember."

Yes, he remembered. "I do not need spirits, thank you. Tea would be lovely."

After ringing for a tray, she began her discourse on every notable death, marriage and birth. He had read most of them in the papers already, but he humoured her. She began with the birth of her grandson and he soon struggled to pay attention.

"…then there was that dreadful boating accident where Lord and Lady Hawthorne drowned."

Luke's ears came to attention. "The Marquess?"

"Yes. It occurred a few months ago. Awful business. He left no heir and the brother inherited."

"I had not heard."

She moved on to the elopement of Lord Worth's youngest with a footman…

And the unfortunate spots on Lady Cassandra's complexion…

Then, how Cunningham lost his hunting box at the gaming tables…

Luke could ask no more without his godmother's perceptive instincts honing in, but he had to hope there was no word of Meg having gone missing or her ladyship would have mentioned it then—if Meg was truly Hawthorne's daughter.

At least there was still a chance she was not ruined. If only he was assured of her safety.

Taking his leave after promising to attend her costumed party in a fortnight, he escaped as quickly as was decent. Walking home with a lighter step, he did not even notice the pains in his leg. It was the first glimmer of optimism he'd had in days, and he could not wait to get home and look in *Debrett's Peerage* for the first time in his remembrance.

MEG WAS grateful for a reprieve from the kitchen, and enjoyed the few moments to be herself again. It was not long-lived. They heard the front door open, followed by boots stamping up the stairs. Meg began to look around in panic for a place to hide.

"Behind the chair, quickly!" Tobin commanded in a harsh whisper. Meg ducked down behind one of the armchairs and prayed her skirts were not peeping out into view. Then the door burst open and someone entered as if in a hurry. Had she been found out?

"Tobin? This is the last place I expected to find you," the Duke teased as he walked toward a shelf on the far wall. He was close enough that she would be discovered if he moved six inches further. Something changed when this man came into the room. Unruly dark locks and languid grace softened his height and broad shoulders. The room suddenly seemed small, his presence taking over as she assimilated a whiff of vetiver and perhaps sandalwood.

"I could say the same of ye, *yer Grace*. Not tha' I would, it bein' yer house. Was yer mission successful?"

"That remains to be seen. Where is the Debrett's book about the peerage?"

"On the table, here."

The Duke looked over and raised his eyebrows. Tobin shrugged his shoulders. Meg would have laughed if she were not so afraid. It was rather comical that he was looking for her and she was hiding right in front of him...except it was not a game. As she watched him studying the pages with intent, she realized he was so very different from Mr. Thurgood. Maybe he did mean to help. If only they had met in different circumstances... The thought gave her pause.

The Duke began flipping through the pages of the book with greater urgency. Saying a silent prayer of thanks she'd had the forethought to shut the book, Meg watched anxiously.

He drummed his finger on a page and read aloud to his henchman. She could make out a few words.

"Richard-Howe 6th Marquess...married Frances...had issue...no heir...Margaret Louise...Amelia Anne... of Hawthorne Abbey, Humberside."

Meg had to bite on her fist to remain quiet. How had he discovered her name so quickly? Why did this Duke care so much? Theirs had only been a brief meeting, for Heaven's sake! He was going to ruin everything!

"How did ye come by tha'? Ye are certain it is she?" Tobin asked.

"Lady Crewe," he said, by way of explanation. The name meant nothing to Meg, though she felt a pang of jealousy on hearing he had spent the afternoon with another woman. What utter nonsense!

"Didn't ye say she was an old harridan?"

Meg relaxed a little.

"That is putting it mildly," the Duke said with a dismissive gesture.

"So ye think our Meg is a fine lady?" Tobin asked in a tone of curiosity. He was quite good at this subterfuge.

Meg was surprisingly touched by the possessiveness both men seemed to feel over her.

"I am almost certain. My esteemed godmother mentioned an unfortunate boating accident in which both Lord and Lady Hawthorne perished. Fortunately, she mentioned no rumours regarding the offspring, hence my anxiety to look in this tome. Here it says Hawthorne left no heir but two daughters, which fits perfectly."

"I suppose Margaret could be shortened to the pet name, Meg," Tobin pretended to ponder. He was walking the fence between both loyalties nicely, but she had little doubt where his true loyalties lay.

"Precisely," the Duke said. "Now, to look in the news-sheets and then I will go to my club to enquire if the new Hawthorne is in Town. I knew the father a little from my brief time in London. He seemed a decent sort."

Meg felt sad at the mention of her papa. A lump formed in her throat, and she had to fix her attention on her breathing to keep quiet.

"How did she fall into the clutches of one as rotten as Thurgood?" Tobin asked.

"That is what I mean to find out. Although that is not as important as ensuring her safety."

"Ye don't think it will raise some eyebrows if ye appear, asking about his missing niece?"

Yes it would! Meg wanted to scream. It could put Amelia in danger!

"I will see what I can learn without asking too many questions," the Duke replied.

"And I will see what I can gather from the servants' quarters myself," Tobin announced.

"Are you staying occupied? If you are unhappy here, you need only say the word if you would rather have a place as a steward or in one of my stables."

Tobin cast a scathing look at the Duke and Meg almost giggled. The Irishman was such an enigma!

The Duke stepped closer into her view, and Meg shamelessly

admired the figure he presented in his buckskins and riding boots, although, when he limped the first few steps, she winced and felt intense guilt for his injury. It must be paining him very much, yet he did not seem to complain. There must be something she could do to make up for the enormous bother she was causing.

He stopped and turned back before he exited the room. "I promised Lady Crewe I would attend her costumed garden party. Please remind me to acquire appropriate attire. She suggested King Henry."

"A party in the garden wearin' hose and a skirt? The Brothers would have a heyday seeing ye thus!" Tobin guffawed.

The Duke gazed at the ceiling. "I am happy to know I provide you with so much amusement. For a moment I almost felt bad for you being confined here in London."

Meg watched with awe at the interchange between duke and batman. They were obviously close. She had never seen her father act thus with any of his servants. It made her wonder about this man and envy the attachment between the two.

"I will dine at the club so that I may find out more but I do not expect to be late."

Tobin nodded as the Duke left. They waited until his footsteps receded down the hallway before blowing out relieved breaths at the same time.

"That was close."

"Too close," he agreed. "What is yer plan now?"

"I suppose I might as well wait to see if my uncle is in Town. If the wedding has not happened yet, Amelia might be here."

"True," he agreed begrudgingly, "but what can ye do about it? He is her guardian now, is he not?"

She slumped into the chair she has been hiding behind. "Unfortunately. And mine for three more months."

"Ye are goin' to need someone powerful to help. I think ye must face the fact tha' ye need my master's connections. If ye cannot see now how obsessed by yer welfare he is, I don't know what would convince ye."

"It is astonishing. I do not pretend to understand why. You may be right, but I need to think about it. I believe he would feel it necessary to marry me and I cannot do that to someone who has been so kind."

"The ways of swells is so strange. Ye haven't even spoken while here, yet if anyone knew ye had been here ye would be forced to marry."

"And if word gets out I ran away, I would also be ruined. It would not matter for most other levels of society?"

"Nay. Ye could go to Ireland and start again. I do have a sister there 'twould welcome ye," he added with pragmatism.

"Become a cousin in truth?" She laughed.

"Why not?" he asked, eyes wide.

"Why not, indeed? Perhaps it will be necessary, but first, I need to see my sister safe. I must return to the kitchens now. I will think on what you said about his Grace. If I can think of a way without him feeling he has compromised me, then I might speak to him."

She thought hard as she made her way back downstairs through the servants' corridors. Could she arrange to meet the Duke without him realizing she was living under his roof? How many lies would she have to tell to protect him?

CHAPTER 8

*W*alking to his club had not been his brightest idea in his almost thirty years. Luke had not covered two streets before the pain became too great and he decided to hail a hackney cab. How many times had he walked this path before without realizing how blessed he was? Too many times. It was pitiful to ride the short distance, but necessary for a while. It would do no good to martyr himself at this point. Greeting the major-domo as he walked through the large wooden door, he handed him his hat but kept his cane for support.

He walked into the drawing room of the new Guards' Club, where some fellow officers sat in comfortable armchairs discussing military strategies and what Napoleon's next move would be, while others played cards and some smoked. A large fire roared at the opposite end of the room, and a large window looked out on to Pall Mall for those who wished to ogle any unfortunates who might pass. Luke felt some weight lift from his shoulders. He had not realized until this moment how difficult it would be to go from major to duke. No one who had not been in boots on the battlefield could truly understand what it was like, even if they were sympathetic. Even knowing he was home and safe, there would forever be a mental separation from soldier and civilian.

Greeting a few familiar faces, who were also home because of injuries, he sat down to attempt casual conversation as he eased into a chair and ordered a brandy plus all of the news-sheets available. Most soldiers cared very little for frivolous society, having been through the harsh realities of an army campaign. For a moment, it was easy to fall back into the role of Major Waverley. He had a new campaign now, though, for he at last recognized the search for Meg for what it was.

Finding her gave him something useful to do. Not that tending to his estates was not useful, but for the most part his stewards could manage. They had done so for two years without him. Sitting and listening to the others' conversations while scanning the papers, he realized there would be little to glean at a military club. Perhaps White's would be more the thing for his purpose. He decided to finish his drink and be on his way.

The news-sheets were disappointing and offered very little information. He supposed, unless there was a great scandal, it was possible to keep your name out of the papers—assuming the new Marquess was staying out of Society because of mourning. Perhaps it would spare Lady Amelia from having to wed too soon. Why, then, had Lady Margaret been sold?

As he finished his drink, he thought he overheard a mention of Hawthorne. Was he hearing what he wanted to? He relaxed back into his high-back chair to listen.

"He came into the title unexpectedly, a few months past. A more undeserving man, I cannot imagine."

Who had come into the title? *Repeat his name,* Luke silently commanded.

"Better off the battlefield, at least," one of the men said. "Limits his scope of damage."

"I thought his men would hand him to the Frogs themselves."

"They probably would have done if he had not sold out for the title."

Luke wracked his brain, but was unaware of anyone who had

recently sold out because of inheriting a title. There were some officers who were hated, to be sure, but a lord?

"After he was publicly shamed at Vitoria for allowing his men to
plunder, it was rather convenient he happened upon a title so soon."

"And he was only acting in Colonel Henry's stead!"

"I wish I would come into a title. I am deuced bored and don't
much care for half-pay." Several men bemoaned their agreement.

"Speaking of, Blake would not have been able to support his habit
at the tables on half-pay," said an older officer Luke recognized from
the House Guards.

"Maybe his brother was tired of paying his debts?" a young captain
suggested. He had perhaps imbibed too much to have voiced such a
statement aloud, Luke thought with a wry twist of his lips.

"Are you suggesting...?"

Luke looked up from his paper to see the captain shrug. It was a
dangerous thought to have spoken out loud, though clearly they all
had been considering the possibility.

Luke knew precisely who Blake was and could hazard a guess as to
why Meg had been sold to Thurgood. If Major Blake truly was
Hawthorne now, it made the situation far more complicated. Luke
could not hear the name without feeling revulsion. However, it might
give him something with which to bargain. How he wished one of his
fellow brothers was here to ask for advice! Tobin would have to do for
now, but he seemed reluctant, for him, to involve himself in this task.
Philip had been the one to work closest to Blake, perhaps he could
write to him for more information. At least being a duke had some
advantages—he could make certain Philip received his letter.

MEG STOPPED before entering the kitchens and returned to her room
instead. She pulled from beneath her bed the gown Mrs. Martin had
handed to her on her way out of the posting house. As Meg unfolded
her lavender muslin, she wondered if it would do or if she could
possibly find some new trimmings. In order to succeed at the decep-

tion and convince the Duke she was unharmed, she needed to look like a lady. She would have to ask Cook or Mrs. Simms for help. Tobin seemed to be willing, but would he know where to go for trimmings, gloves and slippers?

She sat down on the bed, wavering between resolution and reluctance. Could she pull it off? It felt so wrong to deceive this man, but she had been schooled well enough to know he would feel an obligation to her. Why he wished to help was still unfathomable to her, since he knew nothing about her. Still, she owed him so much—some of which he knew nothing about.

Meg made up her mind. She would dress as herself, call on the Duke and beg him to cease looking for her. If her uncle found out, he would also cause trouble for Luke. She did not know if Uncle was yet aware that she had run away from the American merchant, and if so, he must be keeping it quiet for now. After all, pride cometh before honour with Uncle Irving. How had her parents not known his true character? He had been in the army, so one would have thought—perhaps it had changed him.

A loose plan in mind, she went back down the stairs. Entering the kitchen, she knew she would have to enlist more help from the servants who had become dear to her. In fact, she had confided her story to Cook.

"Did you find what you needed, Meg?" Cook enquired while beating some eggs in a bowl.

"Not precisely. I hope to know more by this evening. Mr. Tobin is going to see if he can find out if my uncle is in Town."

Cook gave her a pitying look. "Try not to worry, my dear. I know it is hard but we have to trust that things will work out as they should."

"Tobin thinks I need to speak with his Grace."

"I must say that I agree. He is a good man and would help you."

"I am coming to see that," she said, "but he cannot know I am living under his roof. It would make everything much more complicated and also force his hand. And when my uncle finds out I thwarted his plans..." She shivered in reaction.

"What if you could meet with the Duke and him not know you were living here, like?"

"I considered putting on my only dress and calling on him," she confessed, "but there are so many flaws with that plan. My dress was near ruined by the Channel water and I do not have any way to improve upon it. My hair looks a fright and I have no maid to style it. Where am I supposed to tell him I am staying when he asks?"

"There, there, stop fretting. Where is this dress you speak of?" She wiped her hands on a towel and took off her soiled apron.

"In the attics," Meg answered.

"Let me have a look at it and see if it can be saved." Meg followed the cook up the two flights to her small room in the attic. There was a single bed with a multicoloured patchwork coverlet, a wooden chair and a washing-stand. She picked up the bundle Mrs. Martin had wrapped it in, not wanting to leave it out in case someone should see it. Her fine cloak hung on a hook, but she could always say an employer had gifted it to her. It was more difficult to mistake the quality of the dress, however. She untied the cloth and pulled the lavender confection out. It unfurled and Cook gasped appreciatively.

"It was ruined in the water, I am afraid," Meg said, fingering the ribbon that had taken on a drab hue after her soaking in the sea. Mrs. Martin had managed to clean the linen better than Meg had expected.

"We can change the ribbons on this and make it almost as good as new," Cook said, looking thoughtful while she ran her fingers around the trim.

"Is there somewhere I can go to purchase ribbons without being noticed?

"You leave that to me. How soon do you need this?"

"I only await its refurbishment to speak to his Grace. I cannot call on him as myself looking like this, and if he realizes I am living here, I think he will be quite angry."

"It's rare to see the master in a taking. He was always a good lad. Not that he did not always look for adventure and get into mischief like any other boy."

"You were with him as a child?"

She nodded. "He brought me with him when he inherited. I would not have been French enough for his cousin, the previous Duke. Not wanting to speak ill of the dead, but he got his just deserts...went and got himself killed in a duel." She clicked her tongue.

"Goodness, he sounds like my uncle."

Cook looked at her with sympathy as she held up the gown. "I will be taking this to my sister. My niece wants to be a lady's maid. I will see if she can dress your hair."

"Will it not be remarked upon, to bring her here?"

"Susie comes to visit me often enough. Tomorrow is the servants' afternoon off so it should be easier to see her here unnoticed."

"I do not know if I can do this," Meg said, "but it seems I do not have a choice."

"You can do it for your sister, if nothing else. Now, don't you worry about a thing. I will have this sent to my sister's and then we need to finish the servants' dinner for tonight. His Grace is dining at his club, so it will be a more relaxing evening with only the servant's table to set."

Meg went to her small table and picked up a few coins, then pressed them into Cook's hand. "I only hope it will be enough."

Cook re-wrapped the gown gingerly in the broadcloth it had been wrapped in and carried it back down the stairs. Meg hoped Tobin would return with some good news for her, then maybe she could avoid speaking with the Duke altogether.

CHAPTER 9

*T*he next morning, Tobin brought in Luke's shaving water and began laying out his clothing for the day. Luke had moved on to White's for dinner and had played cards, hoping men would loosen their tongues after a few drinks. It seemed the new Hawthorne was not yet known. Perhaps his disgrace at Vitoria had not yet become common knowledge in London Society. It had been but a few months, and Wellington's dispatch mentioning the plundering disgrace of the 18th Hussars had not called Blake out by name. There was no word of Lady Margaret or Amelia, and Luke had even taken the time to peruse the betting books. How could she have disappeared into thin air?

Luke was so lost in his thoughts, he did not at first register what his batman was asking.

"Beg pardon, Tobin. What was the question?"

"Where would a gent go to purchase fripperies for a lady?" Tobin asked in the same manner he would request an extra piece of bread or a pint of ale.

"I beg your pardon?"

"It was just a question!" Tobin held out his hands defensively.

"Is this why you have been acting strangely since our return? Are you hiding a secret *tendre* for someone?"

"*Leathcheann*," he muttered as he picked up the razor and glared.

"Is that a no or something more sinister?" Luke chuckled. "I am glad I shave myself. You look as though you would slice my throat without a second thought."

"I would think twice," Tobin retorted. "What if I want to buy my sister and mam some nice gloves or a bonnet?"

"How would I know?"

"Do ye not pay the bills for yer mam and sister?"

"Very likely. I can ask Graham."

"Do not bother. I will do it. I must go out for a while."

"Very well." Luke narrowed his gaze. "Why did you not say what you were about in the first place? The London air must be getting to your head, Tobin."

"Perhaps it is. I am to go shopping this morning."

Luke did not bother to reply. His mind was still on Hawthorne and it occurred to him he should warn Tobin. "I found out who the new Hawthorne is."

"Why do I think I will not want t' ken?"

"It is Major Blake." Luke hated to ever mention the name in Tobin's presence again, but it would help him realize the urgency with which they needed to find Meg.

"*Bodalán*," Tobin whispered, making an effort to keep his face impassive, but the twitch beneath his eye and his white knuckles on the chair gave him away. "Poor Meg," he muttered as he turned to clean up Luke's shaving instruments.

"Have you heard more since…you left his service?" Luke leaned against the door frame, holding his neckcloth.

Tobin snorted. "Making free with villagers' innocent daughters, a hundred lashes for small offences, gambling with those that could ill afford it…" Tobin did not need to remind Luke what he had done to him.

"The army is much better off with him gone, though we knew that. I would like to know the precise date he was discharged."

70

"Why does it matter?"

"Because I think he killed Meg's parents."

"Go n-ithe an cat thú is go n-ithe an diabhal an cat!"

"My sentiments, I am sure." He should learn to speak Gaelic. Luke would swear he heard cat and devil in there and had no idea how that equalled a curse, but he was sure it did.

"There is not anythin' anyone can do, is there? He wasn't tried for crimes in the army and now he is more untouchable, isn't he? He was no better than slapped on the wrist and sent home."

Luke was certain Tobin would have spat if they were outside. He was grateful for the restraint.

"Unless Meg's parents met their demise by his hand, which would be most difficult to prove at this point. Although a hint dropped in an ear could do considerable damage to his reputation. However, that could harm Meg and her sister as well."

"No wonder she does not wish to return home."

"It is much worse than I had originally thought. I have no idea how else to find her. We have done everything we know. How helpless she must feel!" Luke looked down at the cloth now twisted in his hands and threw it down.

"I imagine she will try to contact her sister if she can." Tobin handed him a fresh neckcloth. "Could ye try to speak with her and see if she is safe? I cannot see Hawthorne treating the girl any better."

"If the family is in mourning, they will not be attending Society events this year." Luke tied his neckcloth in a simple barrel-knot.

"Are ye goin' to offer to marry the girl instead?"

"What use do I have with a young girl? It is a valid point, however; I will think of something."

This was met with more muttering.

"For now, I will have Graham investigate the circumstances surrounding the previous Hawthorne death. I believe we might need to send Runners to Humberside."

"I think ye are goin' t' have two ladies on yer hands if ye are not careful, yer Grace." Tobin's voice was light, but the admonition was still there.

"I suppose that is better than their current fate." He dismissed the warning with a shrug.

"Ye cannot save everyone."

"I can try," he snapped and exited the room. Tobin was right, curse him, but he could not let this matter go.

Practically storming down the stairs as best his sore leg would allow, he was in a foul temper. If only his wounds were healed, he would take a look in at Gentleman Jackson's and vent his anger appropriately. Instead, he directed Graham to hire some Runners and then spent the day in his study, brooding.

JUMPING from the ship had been easy in comparison to facing the Duke. Meg knew she needed his help, but it was not right to ask it of him—she had no claim on his honour. Her conscience kept talking her out of it, but she had no money and nowhere else to go. She was actually content in his household as a cook. She never would have believed it possible before.

All of her free hours had been spent with how to rescue her sister. It would be some time before she would have enough money to purchase her own ticket to Oxford on the stage. Once she was there, would she be able to take Amelia away? Much though her thoughts were consumed by this, she could think of no other way. Unfortunately, Amelia would be forced to work as well, in order to keep them off the streets, or she would have to stay where she was until Meg came into her inheritance. Would it be too late by then?

How she wished she could prove her uncle had harmed her parents on purpose, but she had no such evidence, only a deep conviction. There was a soft knock on her door, interrupting her cogitations, and she jumped up from her bed to answer it.

Cook stood there with a pretty young girl about Amelia's age, if Meg guessed correctly. Cook was practically beaming with excitement. "This is Susie." The girl bobbed a curtsy but said nothing.

"Are you ready, Miss Meg?" Cook held up the dress, which had been draped over her arm, and unfurled it for her approval. It had been restored to its original beauty.

"Oh, Cook! You have outdone yourself!"

"Yes, I have," she said with a wink. "We will help you put on your stays and Susie, here, can dress your hair. I've sent Tobin after gloves and slippers and I expect him back soon. The master has been in his study all day, so tea would be a good time to call."

Meg allowed herself to be helped into her stays and then sat obediently in the small wooden chair. Susie was remarkably proficient at dressing hair, and Meg vowed, if she ever escaped this situation, she would remember to hire her. Susie managed to form her curls into a loose knot and leave enough dangling to soften the look. Meg glanced appreciatively in the small looking-glass above the washing-stand. Cook and Susie then helped her into her dress and tightened the laces.

There was a knock on the door and Cook answered it to reveal Tobin standing in the opening, looking much put upon. Meg had to hide a laugh behind her hand. He stopped when he saw her.

"Beggorah," Tobin whispered under his breath, his eyes glowing with appreciation.

"It ain't nice to speak how people can't understand you," Cook chastised.

"I suppose ye will need these t' complete yer look," he said to Meg, ignoring Cook.

Handing her a package, she unwrapped it and gasped with surprise. "Tobin, I cannot believe you managed this!"

Pulling out a pair of slippers and new black kid gloves, she put them on. "You have even remembered my being in mourning," she said with astonishment.

"Cook reminded me to," he confessed. "I had never seen ye completely undisguised before. Ye do look a lady, in truth."

"Are you certain this is the right thing to do, too? I do not know what the Duke will be able to accomplish. My uncle is a very unpredictable man."

"If anyone can help, 'tis my master. What can it hurt t' ask?"

"A great deal," she muttered.

"I will take ye to the drawin' room and tell him he has a caller."

Cook began to hurry out of the door. "I will send tea up."

"Cook," Meg called after her, "thank you for everything."

Cook waved away the praise and continued on down the stairs. Meg turned to Susie and also expressed her appreciation. The girl bobbed a proper curtsy, apparently still too shy to say much.

Following Tobin down the stairs, Meg tried to take deep breaths in order to steady her nerves. He showed her into a drawing room, and she wondered if the butler took his half-day with the other servants. If not, someone must have distracted him in order to help her carry off this charade. Sitting on the claret-coloured settee, she looked around and almost felt as if she were back home at Hawthorne Abbey. From the elegantly papered walls to the thick Aubusson carpet, it was much like her mother's drawing room at home. A few moments later, she overheard Tobin tell the Duke he had a caller. Her heart began to pound in her chest and she found her hands were trembling. She had to think of Amelia or she would run from the room in a panic. It was most improper for her to be calling on any man unchaperoned.

"He has been looking for you. He wants to help you," she reminded herself.

Somewhere during her conversation with herself she had risen and she began to pace across the room. Steps echoed in the entrance hall and the door opened. She turned and her eyes met his, midnight blue and questioning. She could see when it suddenly dawned on him who she was.

"Meg? Is it really you?"

"Yes, your Grace." She fell into a deep curtsy, trying to buy herself more time to consider. Now that he was here, it was even harder to think of what to say.

"I have been looking for you." He bowed elegantly.

"Yes, I heard. I have come to beg you to stop."

He looked taken aback by her statement.

"Have you been restored to your family? Can I be assured of your safety? I have found out a great deal about your uncle since last I saw you. Does he know you have escaped Mr. Thurgood?"

Meg had not been prepared for this onslaught of questions. Any gentleman would have said no more at the request to stop, would they not? She should lie to this man and set him free, but something about the concerned look in his eyes kept her from taking that course.

"I do not know," she answered honestly, in a soft voice.

"How can I help you?"

"Why, your Grace? You should not become involved. My uncle is capable of..." She did not know how to explain it. After all, she had no proof he had killed her parents. She turned to stare out of the window, yet saw nothing, for her gaze looked inward.

"You need not elaborate. I am well aware of what he is capable of and that is why I have determined to find you. I will admit, in the beginning, I only wanted to ensure you had found your way to safety; away from an unwanted marriage. Now that I have discovered more, I believe you are in more danger from him than Thurgood."

"He cares nothing for what happens to me, so long as my sister is safe. He still has her and intends to wed her to a rich old lord."

"There could be worse fates."

She turned to disagree. "Not for Amelia. She is so young and innocent and all that is good in this world. She deserves better."

"Forgive my manners. Please sit down. I will ring for tea. I want to know everything, so I may decide how best to help you." A tap came on the door before he could ask for anything, and Tobin walked in with the tea tray, setting it down on a low table in front of Meg. He gave her a slight wink before leaving.

Meg poured the tea, still fighting to keep her hands from trembling. The Duke waved away any milk or sugar and she handed him his cup. Their fingers brushed lightly, and yet she felt a warming tingle all the way to her toes.

She took her own cup, which was liberally dosed with milk and sugar, and sat down again on the edge of her chair, as she had been taught to do.

"Now, let us begin with what I know. Somehow, you escaped Mr. Thurgood's ship, which was to carry you to America. Were you to marry him?"

She traced the floral designs on her tea-cup with her finger. "Yes. He paid my uncle a hundred thousand pounds for that privilege."

"The devil, you say! No wonder he is angry." He ran his fingers through his hair in frustration. "I have made some enquiries about Thurgood, however, and he can well afford the sum."

"He did not receive the goods. He has a right to be angry. Nevertheless, I will not marry against my will to please my uncle."

"And so you shall not."

"I wish I could have such confidence. If only I can remain hidden until my majority in three months, I will at least have my own inheritance."

"I must have encountered you not long after you had escaped the ship, then," he surmised, looking at her with raised brows.

"You are correct, sir. I was hurrying to get away as fast as possible when the ruffians grabbed me. I should have known better than to go straight through the road, but I was wet and very cold and had little awareness of where I was. I am fortunate I awoke before we set sail."

"How could you have known?"

She shook her head. "I have not properly thanked you for saving me."

He inclined his head in silent acknowledgement, as though it was an everyday occurrence. "So, after you escaped the inn, you stopped for the night at Simpson's farm?"

"How did you know?" Meg's cup halted halfway to her lips.

"Fortunately, Mr. Thurgood had stopped there just before us. It was clear to Mrs. Simpson who was the villain in this play. I do not know when he discovered he had been deceived, but he must have guessed as much fairly quickly. He arrived at the posting house not long after I did. That patroness said you had gone on to London and I guessed she, at least, was telling the truth."

Meg was afraid of what his next question would be.

"Have you friends here who are helping you?"

"Yes." Again, she answered as little as possible.

"I am relieved to hear it." He crossed one booted leg over the other and relaxed back into the chair.

He was an imposing figure and Meg was all too aware of his masculinity. It was disconcerting to have all of his attention on her, yet she wondered how it would feel to be so cherished as a wife.

"Please tell me how I may be of assistance."

His eyes were studying her. Could he read her thoughts? She hoped she was not blushing.

"Do you know if my uncle is in Town? I need to find a way to make contact with my sister."

"I will send my man to see. I only discovered yesterday who you were and, therefore, more of your circumstances. It would help, of course, if they are in Town. Even though their mourning prevents most *ton* entertainments, it will be easier to manoeuvre an introduction if they are here."

Meg nodded. He had thought through the matter better than she had. "I cannot openly search for her or I risk my uncle finding me."

"Do you need a place to hide?"

"No, your Grace. I am perfectly safe where I am." It was the truth, at least.

"How may I get word to you if I discover something?"

Trying to think quickly, Meg began to panic. "I do not know. You cannot send me letters where I am. It would not do at all."

"If I placed it in my garden, would you be able to retrieve it? There is a gazebo inside the back gate where I can easily leave messages for you."

"I can come before dawn and remain unseen. That would be very good of you, your Grace."

"May we not go back to your addressing me as Luke? I confess I would prefer it. Unless you want to be Lady Margaret?"

"No! Luke and Meg will do very well."

He smiled for the first time, and in that moment Meg was wistful for what her parents' deaths had caused her to give up. Not long ago it would have been possible for her to dream of meeting a duke like this and waltzing with him at a ball whilst dressed like a princess. Now, she peeled carrots and potatoes. That smile gave her fanciful ideas which she needed to forget.

She stood up quickly and he winced as he also came to his feet.

"Forgive me, your Grace. Does it pain you very much?"

"No. You are not responsible for this pain. That wound has healed very nicely."

"Then why do you hurt so?" It was inappropriate to ask, but the question had left her lips before she had thought better of it.

"I was the unfortunate recipient of some French shrapnel."

What did one say to that? I am sorry? He saved her from speaking trivialities.

"I promise to do what I can, Meg. Promise me you will be safe."

"I am doing my best," she replied while feeling guilty for not telling him the whole truth. "If you discover where my sister is, I would like to find a way to get a letter to her."

"We will think of a way," he said as he took her hand and kissed the air above it. His midnight eyes seared into hers and it was difficult to look away. She felt a fluttering sensation course through her, and her lips began to tingle as his gaze fell upon her lips. Awareness danced up her spine as she forced herself to move towards the door. How tempting it was to take advantage of his gallantry and keep him for herself!

She said her farewells and left by the front door. The interview had gone better than she had expected. Now, all she had to do was sneak around to the servant's entrance without him knowing.

CHAPTER 10

*L*uke watched Meg go and wanted to follow after her. Tobin joined him as, shamelessly, they stood watching from the window. She disappeared around the corner of the house, having once more donned her heavy cape, complete with hood, to hide herself.

"It goes against every fibre of my being not to chase after her and insist she stay here."

"Ye know you cannot do tha', Major."

"She insists she is in a safe place."

"Then ye must trust her."

"She asked me to stop looking for her, but did ask if I might be able to discover whether her uncle and sister are in Town."

"Did she?" Tobin raised his eyebrows as though surprised. "So she agreed to further communication with ye?"

"I am to leave information in the garden for her. She asked for help in getting a letter to her sister."

"I am not surprised. Does she think t' run away with her?"

"She did not say, but I also cannot be sure I would not help her do it," Luke admitted.

Tobin muttered under his breath, as Luke had expected. He pulled his gaze away from the window reluctantly.

"Were you able to discover anything from the tavern?"

"Hawthorne is in Town. He is not well liked—no surprise there. I am fairly certain some of his servants could be bribed, although his valet seemed loyal."

Luke nodded. "Is he newly arrived? I expect he was summoned by Thurgood and brought the girl with him. If that is indeed the case, then Meg is now in more danger. I hope she will heed my advice and allow me to intercede on her behalf."

"Do ye think she will?"

"It is hard to say. She must trust me a little to have come here, but I also sensed some desperation in her manner. She looked as if she were about to walk to the gallows." Luke did not add his questions of how she had found him, but perhaps she had discovered his card whilst he was incapacitated in Portsmouth.

"She might as well, given her current choices," Tobin added dryly.

Luke glared at his man. "If you mean to discourage me, that is not the way."

"I know ye well enough to know ye will see this to its end, no matter if it sees you leg-shackled or fourteen paces away from Hawthorne's pistol."

"Did you see her?" Luke asked, ignoring the previous remark, because again, curse him, his batman had knocked the nail on the head and he did not have a clever retort.

"Aye, she's an angel."

Luke began to pace the edges of the Aubusson carpet, deep in thought. "We could leave this information in the garden as promised, but will she try to approach her uncle herself, or sneak into his house in search of her sister?"

Tobin remained silent.

"We both know what her uncle is capable of, and he must feel untouchable now, as a marquess. And to a large extent, he is."

"She seemed appropriately afraid of him... but I still don't know what ye think ye can do. He is their legal guardian," Tobin argued.

"We have to prove wrong-doing. I think we need to find out more about her parents' accident."

"Ye think he killed them?"

"If not by his own hand, then by his order." Luke just had a nagging feeling. "It was why I sent the Runners. They have an excellent reputation for ferreting out the truth."

"I hope you sent them plenty of coin."

Luke resumed pacing, with his hands clasped behind his back.

Tobin just watched. Fortunately, he was used to Luke's habits when he needed to think. Presently, Luke looked up at Tobin and a question caught in his throat.

"What are ye considerin' now?" his man asked in his forthright way.

"I was thinking of paying a social call on the new Hawthorne, debating whether to play dumb about his brother's demise. We were acquainted, if not very well, but Hawthorne will not be aware of that."

"Would that help anythin'?" Tobin did not look impressed with the idea.

"I was thinking, if I pretended an interest in Lady Margaret, as though his brother and I had discussed the possibility..."

"What if he calls yer bluff? *Go raibh tú pósadh i haste agus repent ag fóillíochta!*" Tobin said to the Heavens with a warning in his voice.

"I have to marry sometime—at least this would be for a good cause." Luke did not know when he had decided, but it seemed like the proper thing to do.

"A braw face has gone to yer head," Tobin said in disbelief. "Are ye willing to pay Thurgood a hundred thousand quid?"

"Meg cannot be forced to marry him against her will according to the law."

"As ye said, he is now above the law. He has never allowed it to stop him before," Tobin snarled. He knew the truth of that statement more than anyone.

"Thurgood can take it up with Hawthorne. It is my word against Hawthorne's that we had an understanding. I cannot think his reputation would survive the scandal."

"Ye do not even know the girl! Her name would be sullied as well."

"I would like to change that if she will allow it. Much can be done to redeem her name with the title duchess," Luke reasoned. He hoped it was true.

"Ye have gone completely stark ravin' mad." Tobin shook his head.

"Very likely. Would you like to go to Bow Street with me?"

"Why not?"

MEG HAD RETURNED to her room to become a kitchen maid once again. It was hard to wait until the next morning for news—if there even was news.

Calling on the Duke had not been as bad as she had anticipated. It was probably the best thing she could have done in the situation. If she went out looking for Amelia herself, it might well land her back in the clutches of Thurgood or her uncle, or she could be attacked again, as she had been the first night. Feeling so helpless was infuriating and she owed so much to the Duke. How could she ever repay him?

Dressed in her disguise except for the glasses, she crept down the back stairs and out into the garden. She had chosen this time because she would not be seen. It was cold in the dark morning when the kitchen servants woke to begin preparing food for the day. Few of the other household servants had to begin work so early.

Her boots crunched on the gravel path as she walked along from the formal gardens to where it was wild and natural. Having been in London a little while now, she understood the luxury of having such gardens in the middle of town. The only other parks that rivaled the Duke's in her opinion were the King's. Not that she had seen many other parks in Town.

Walking with her arms wrapped around her body, she had not brought her cloak for this errand since the kitchens were always suffocatingly warm. Luke had said near the back gate, so she had followed the path as far as she could to the brick wall, yet as she looked around she could see no gazebo.

"Which direction should I go?" She started towards the right, hoping it was the way. Winding through tall birches and oaks she was again reminded of home, even though the air was not as clean.

She had never been to this part of the garden, the servants' entrance being on the side where deliveries were made. This was far from that, and she wished dawn would come a little quicker.

Walking more briskly, she began to grow afraid. It was silly, she knew, but she could not stop an eerie feeling that ambush waited beyond every corner, since that night in Portsmouth. Her thoughts went back to Luke, her Saviour, and where she would be now if he had not stumbled upon them. It almost did not bear thinking about, except she owed him so much. At this point, however, she had to accept his help. Meg was too afraid to confront her uncle before her birthday, at the very least, and only if no other options existed. However, she had to get word to Amelia. Did her sister have any idea what had happened to her elder sibling? Meg had been drugged and stolen, like a thief in the night, without even saying goodbye. Poor Amelia must be terrified! Saying a quick prayer that the Duke would help her pass on a letter, Meg tried to think of what would happen after that. She could not stay here forever. Eventually, he would find out.

Knowing her uncle would only be patient as long as he must, she did not know whether or not he would wed Amelia off quietly as soon as they reached the end of mourning.

Meg and her uncle had had some dreadful rows since he had made known his plans for them, and he had shown his true nature when she had objected. Her body gave a nervous shudder when she remembered that possessed, evil look in his eyes. Worse yet, Amelia was still with him. Fortunately, as long as she was compliant, her uncle would be kind to her. Thinking of her innocent sister deepened her resolve once again.

The tree branches rustled in the wind, and her boots crunched on the frosty earth as she kept searching. Inhaling deeply of the brisk autumn air, the smell of burning wood wafted from the chimneys and she tried not to think of being alone in the dark. She stopped to take stock of her surroundings and felt the hair rise on the back of her neck. Something was there. She froze and debated running back to the house when a mouser cat jumped from a bush and chased after its prey.

Feeling ridiculous at her nerves, she followed the path until at last she spied the white columns of a gazebo which had a pointed roof. Dawn was finally breaking over the horizon and for that she was grateful. She had feared she had been walking in circles.

"Good morning, Meg,"

She screamed.

CHAPTER 11

*L*uke?" She gasped and jumped. "You frightened me!"

"My apologies. I had not intended to alarm you. I decided it would be better to speak to you in person, but I had not realized how dark it would be."

"Yes, I became lost in the garden. It is quite large." Luke almost laughed at how polite she was being.

"You are welcome to seek refuge in it at any time," he added, equally polite.

"Thank you." Her voice trembled. "Did you discover anything?"

"Yes, your uncle is newly arrived in Town. We were unable to determine if your sister is there with him. I imagine we can ascertain that quickly if servants gossip or may be easily bribed."

She wrinkled her nose adorably. "I am not familiar with the London servants. Only a few would travel with Papa when he came for the Sessions. My uncle is very sly and would only bring those he trusted."

"Unless he hired an entirely new household here, of course. However, I hope there will be someone who will be willing to talk."

"I do not think he would have left Amelia in Humberside, especially if he is aware of my escape. He could well be guarding her without her realizing it."

"I suspect the same. Let me continue to investigate, and if you wish to write a letter I should do so, that we may then pass it to her if we find the opportunity."

"Of course. I will attend to it today. Should I leave it here?"

He stared at her long and hard, debating whether to ask her about his suspicions or allow this charade to continue.

"I must be returning before the household awakes," she said, beginning to fuss with the cuffs on her drab grey servant's uniform.

"Meg, how did you get into the garden?" She had not come through the back gate, of that he was sure.

"I came from the servant's entrance," she replied, though her eyes had gone wide.

"Why are you wearing a servant's costume today when you were dressed as a lady yesterday?"

Her chin began to quiver and he felt like a cad.

"I, I..." she began to explain and Luke felt something pull deep inside his chest.

He took her in his arms when the first tear rolled down her cheek. She stiffened before breaking into sobs and clinging to him. It was a nice feeling to have her in his arms, which was a good thing if his suspicions were correct. Not only was she a lady of the highest order, but they had also been alone together, unchaperoned, more than once. Not that anything untoward had happened, but it was seen as good as signing your name in the register, to the high sticklers of Society, if discovered. Not that he ever intended them to find out, but there would be questions if it was publicly known that she had run away, and if it was discovered where she was hiding. Was she even aware of the repercussions of being under his roof? Having led a sheltered life in the country, she might not be aware. His mind raced furiously for the best way to handle this, but for now he felt only relief for her safety. Hawthorne would not dare harm her here.

Meg sobbed until shudders rocked her thin body and she relaxed in his arms. It was a sensation Luke would not soon forget, and he savoured every moment from the way her body melded to his to the clean smell of her plain soap.

He waited for her to speak as he ran his hand soothingly up and down her back, while the other stroked through a few curls which had escaped the knot on her head.

"Are you angry with me for deceiving you?" She looked up at him with those pale blue eyes looking fearful of his response.

"How could I be angry, Meg? I wish you could have trusted me, but I understand why you did not."

"You do? Tobin said you had been looking everywhere for me, which surprised me."

"Tobin knew you were here?" Reluctantly, he let go of Meg and then ran his hands through his hair. She stood there watching him with those large, hunted eyes which had haunted his dreams since he had first met her.

"Of course Tobin knew," he answered his own question. Pieces of the puzzle began to fall into place: Tobin riding in the carriage, the extra rider, the strange behaviour...

She stepped forward and placed her hand on his arm, her attitude pleading. "Please do not be angry with him. I swore him to secrecy and he was not at all pleased. It is quite clear where his loyalties are. I only wish I could speak Gaelic." She laughed and gave the most enchanting half-smile which also revealed a dimple. He had an immediate impulse to kiss it. In that moment he knew she could have asked for the world and he would have given it to her.

"We must decide what to do next."

"Can we not continue in the same manner?" she asked innocently.

"You cannot be a servant in my home!" He had raised his voice and she shied away. Closing his eyes, he shook his head. "Forgive me, Meg. I did not mean to raise my voice."

She hugged her body with her arms and walked to the edge of the stone steps. Standing between two columns, she looked out at the gardens.

"Cook will be expecting me. Please do not make me leave. I do not know where else I will go."

"You will go nowhere. You are safest here with me. Hawthorne would not dare to cross me or it would mean social ruin."

"Only if you promise to feel no obligation towards me. I am no longer a lady. I knew what I was about before I jumped from the ship."

Luke did not want to promise any such thing, but he would, because it would not be an obligation. However, he realized he would have to convince her of that. "I promise I will feel no obligation."

She nodded with what looked like relief and began to walk away. Was the thought of becoming his Duchess so abhorrent, or did she fear he would not want her?

How could she have been so stupid? In disbelief she walked back to the kitchens and sat on a stool, her head drooping.

"Well, I know you did not steal the biscuits, so what has you looking so glum?" Cook asked as she turned some bacon in a pan.

"He knows," she answered simply.

Cook frowned, clearly trying to discern what she was saying. No doubt she was not making any sense, but she was so upset with herself, the words were not forming properly. At last, it dawned on Cook. "The Duke found you out?" she asked in a loud whisper as she stirred something in a bowl she held tucked under one arm.

Meg nodded and she knew her face wrinkled in the most ugly fashion, but what was she to do now? She had seen the machinations going on in his head by the look in his eyes. He had something in mind, of that she was sure.

"Was he angry?" Cook continued in a conspiratorial tone.

"If he was, he hid it well. He is far too kind—or adept at hiding his feelings. I must find somewhere to go, quickly, where he will not find me this time." Or where she would grow too comfortable and make the same mistake, she added silently.

"Now how will that be any better? You have found a safe place and that is no guarantee elsewhere," Cook said in a motherly tone. She was almost scolding.

"As Tobin keeps reminding me, his Grace's sense of chivalry is so great that his conscience would not permit him to do anything but search for me. I could see in his eyes that he was considering how to save my reputation." Meg shook her head.

"Then leave it up to him, I say, if he is going to all this trouble anyway."

"He will think it necessary to marry me, or at the very least create an elaborate scheme to avoid scandal."

"There are worse things than being his Duchess, I'm sure." The kind woman continued to scold.

"I am not unmindful of the honour it would be. Before my parents' death, it might have been possible to dream, but I have not yet reached my majority and my uncle owes the American merchant a great deal of money. What a brumble-broth we are in, and I cannot endanger his Grace."

Cook put her bowl down and placed her hands on her hips before looking Heavenward in a show of exasperation.

"That is why it is fortunate indeed you crossed his Grace's path. If anyone can save you now it is he. I do not think it a coincidence."

"I have become his servant!" she said a little too loudly, causing other servants to glance their way as they gathered for their breakfast.

Cook clicked her tongue. "No one will blame you for doing what you've done. Anyone with honour would have done the same."

Meg did not believe Society would be so understanding. It played by a different set of rules. Trying to explain this to a servant, however, would do her no good.

If Cook would not help her, she would have to find something on her own. Unless...

"What are you planning over there?"

"Nothing yet," she said, taking some bread dough and beginning to knead it. While she took her frustrations out on the poor mound of dough, her mind flickered about, thinking of options. Tobin would help. He had Luke's best interests at heart and would not want him forced into a marriage with her or scandal tied to his name.

89

Forming her dough into the shapes of loaves, she placed them in the waiting pans and covered them with a cloth to be set to rise.

"Cook, I will need to go out today. I realize it is not my half day, but as I cannot stay here, I must look for another place."

The motherly woman did not look pleased. "I cannot talk you out of it?"

"If I am discovered my uncle will force me, no matter who protects me. I cannot imagine what he would do to the Duke—he would not hesitate to challenge him. It will be better for everyone if I leave."

"Everyone except you."

Yes, there was that, she concurred. She had grown very comfortable here in a short time and the contentment of Luke's arms was something she would never forget. It was more than safety—it was having her own knight errant prepared to slay dragons on her behalf. That feeling would have to carry her dreams for a very long time. Even if she survived this situation without having to wed Thurgood, she would still be fortunate if she could afterwards hide somewhere and pretend to be a widow.

"Could you please have someone send Tobin to help me?" She took off her apron and hung it on a hook. She was not needed in the kitchens anyway. Cook had pretended to find her something to do. It had given her much time to think and had provided safety, and now she was to be on her own again.

Climbing the stairs to her small room in the attic, she threw her spectacles and mob-cap on the bed, then pulled out the broadcloth in which Mrs. Martin had packed her gown. She began placing her possessions inside, remembering fondly the short time yesterday when she had been herself again. Tears streamed down her face, but that was the only display of sorrow she allowed herself. She wiped them away as she heard a soft knock on the door.

Meg opened the door to find Tobin standing there and allowed herself to droop with relief. Forgetting she was the lady was not so hard, after all.

"What is the matter, *mo chara*?" Tobin asked with concern.

She looked into the hallway from side to side, then, ensuring no one was about, pulled him inside. Most of the servants had gone downstairs to begin their duties, but she could not be too careful.

"The Duke was there this morning when I went to look for a letter. He surmised that I am staying here!"

Tobin sank into the chair and looked relieved. *"Buíochas le Dia,"* he declared with clear sentiment.

"How can you say that? I thought you, of all people, would understand!"

"What I understand is the Major is not goin' to let this matter rest no matter where ye are. The way I see it, if he knows yer here, it will be less stressful for him."

She shook her head violently. "I will leave him a note, begging him to cease this at once. My uncle is a cruel man. He will call him out at the very least, and with my being under the Duke's roof…"

Tobin interrupted. "I know, I know ye think he will be forced to marry ye."

She put her hands on her hips and gave him her fiercest look of disapproval. He did not seem impressed.

"I no longer see him havin' to marry ye as the worst thing in the world."

She felt her jaw drop, allowing her mouth to gape open.

"As for yer uncle, we are all too familiar with him. He was sent home from the army in shame, in June. Did ye know that?"

"June," she repeated, in barely a whisper.

"Aye," he continued, his voice menacing. "He is one of the most loathed officers. Finding out he did this to ye was no great surprise at all."

She hardly heard anything after he said 'June'. She sat on the edge of her bed. "So it could have been him."

"Go dtachta an diabhal thu, Hawthorne!" Tobin swore. "Miss Meg, may I have yer word that ye will not leave?"

"I cannot give it. I would be lying. If you will not help me, I will manage on my own."

"Then ye will become a prisoner here, because I owe tha' to my master, at least. I was glad enough to help ye when ye were content to

91

stay safe here, but ye do not realize what could happen to ye beyond these walls and what it will do to my master."

"I realize the dangers," she said thinking back to the very first night. "I am doing this for him."

"Then don't," he argued. "Give me yer word ye will not leave or I will lock ye in until I can speak with him."

"How dare you! How can you think this is best for him?" she argued.

"Because he will never leave it be."

Meg jumped up from the bed and began to pace about the tiny room. What was already a disaster was taking on epic proportions. Trying to argue with this stubborn Irishman was worse than trying to beat a brick wall. She puffed out her cheeks and blew out a breath of frustration. Glaring at him, she reluctantly agreed. "Only until we decide upon a better plan."

"Fair enough. I will return when I've spoken to him." He hurried out of the door and she heard the key turn in the lock before she realized what he was about.

CHAPTER 12

*L*uke sat in the garden for a long time after Meg had walked away, deep in thought. He was utterly befuddled. She had been under his nose the whole time! If he went into the house now he was liable to thrash Tobin, so he stayed where he was and pondered his next move.

Now that he did not have to waste time searching for Meg, he could focus his energy on how to deal with Hawthorne. Thurgood was of little concern to him, and Luke smiled at the thought of that braggart dealing with the new Marquess. Luke suspected Hawthorne had already spent the money paid for Meg. But how best to deal with this situation in order to protect Meg and Amelia's reputations?

On the thought, he rose to pen a letter to his mother. If she arrived quickly and quietly, no one except three trusted servants would know when Meg arrived for certain. As he walked back through the gardens, the sunrise put on a most glorious display of lavender and pink, as though blessing what was to come. A sense of peace came over him, and he did not fear the bonds of marriage as he had once thought he would. In fact, he rather enjoyed the idea of Meg by his side forever. He could only hope the idea was not abhorrent to her. He was a slight improvement on Thurgood, he thought wryly.

Perhaps half an hour later, having added a quick note to the Archbishop and one to the Prince Regent, begging an audience, he was sanding and sealing all three missives when Tobin burst through the door of Luke's study. His batman looked greatly concerned, and any thoughts of knocking him unconscious dissipated.

"I have locked Meg in her room. The chit is maddenin'," he announced.

For a moment, Luke was stunned into speechlessness. "I beg your pardon? Did you just say you have locked my future duchess in her room?"

"Aye. She was threatenin' to leave!" He held out his hands defensively.

Luke stood up, with the letters he had written in his hand, and took them out to his butler, instructing him to have them delivered in all haste. He returned to his study and closed the door behind him, leaning against it as he tried to assimilate what Tobin had said.

This is not what he had expected. Another brisk knock sounded on the door behind him. Turning to open it, he found Cook standing there, looking harassed. He stepped aside and directed her to come in. Closing the door again, he walked over to his desk and leaned against it.

"Do you need something, Cook?"

She bobbed a curtsy before beginning her exclamations. "Oh, your Grace! I know I'm betraying Miss Meg's confidence, but I fear she will run away. I've been fretting since she told me," she said, wringing her apron between her hands. She was clearly disturbed.

"You did the right thing in coming to me," he reassured her. "What did she say to you?"

"Only that she must find another place in order to protect you. It seems she thinks you will feel an obligation to her and that her uncle will harm you." Her cheeks reddened as she spoke.

Meg understood very well, then, what the implications were. How could he convince her to stay? "Thank you for telling me, Cook. You were quite right to do so."

She nodded with visible relief and bobbed a second curtsy before hurrying back out of the room. As she left, Mrs. Simms appeared and Luke could only imagine what she had to say. Meg had made quite an impression on his trusted retainers, it seemed, in a short time.

"Good morning, Mrs. Simms. Have you news for me as well?"

"I have an idea of what is afoot and assumed you would have instructions for me." she replied with dignity.

Luke accepted the mild rebuke for intimating his housekeeper was a gossip and smothered a mischievous grin. He dared not look at Tobin.

"Indeed. Lady Laurence will be joining us by tomorrow at the latest, and I would like a guest chamber prepared for Lady Margaret. We will not announce her presence to the household until Lady Laurence arrives and she can be known as her guest."

"I assumed as much, your Grace." She broke out in one of her rare smiles. "May I say, I will be delighted to have Lady Margaret as our new mistress." She dropped a curtsy and left.

"It seems Meg's fears were well-founded," he said out loud, wondering if all retainers would be so bold as to speak to him thus— not that he would want it any other way.

"May I suggest you speak to her presently? I am not going within a mile of her until I have to—and not before this day is out."

"I will go." He held out his hand for the key, which Tobin released as though it was a hot coal. Luke laughed. "May I suggest, as your penance, you ponder how we are to deal with Hawthorne?"

Tobin grunted. "A cat 'o nine tails and a noose is too good fer him," he muttered.

"I could approach him at his club. I also considered whether it would be wise to join forces with Thurgood against the Marquess."

"Join that blackguard?"

"He has every right to be angry for being duped, but when I explain that Meg is my intended and not Hawthorne's to sell, he will redirect his ire appropriately."

"Ye give him too much credit."

"Perhaps." He sighed and walked to the door. "It is the best I can come up with, so I welcome your ideas," he said, leaving Tobin cursing in Gaelic as he began his way up to the attics. Dealing with Thurgood and Hawthorne might be the simplest task he faced. He had not anticipated such resistance from Meg. Nevertheless, he had once been lauded by his fellow brothers-in-arms as being able to turn the ladies up sweet. By turning on his supposed charm, he would do his best to convince her that being his duchess would be a complete pleasure.

MEG HEARD footsteps approaching and debated her options. She wanted to bang on the door and scream for her release, but knew it would be unlikely any of the servants would defy the Duke. Instead, she stayed on her bed, prostrate, at the mercy of Tobin and his Grace. The confident steps grew louder, and she lifted her head when the key turned in her door. There was a knock. Did gaolers typically knock?

"Come in," she replied, furious at the weakness of her voice.

Luke opened the door and stood on the threshold. No doubt he was waiting to see if she would throw something at him. Their eyes met and the look he gave her made her feel warm and tingly all over. She sat up briskly, feeling vulnerable on the bed. He held out his hand and she rose and came to him, placing her reddened fingers in his far larger palm. The strength of it was both exciting and unnerving. Silently, he led her down some stairs onto the floor below. She kept her head down, watching her boots travel along the plush blue carpet, and hoping no one else was about.

"This will be your new room," he opened a door to show her, before walking on past three more doors. She did not bother to protest.

Entering what looked to be a private chamber, he closed the door and led her to a table with two chairs. Breakfast for two had been laid out in what appeared to be a sitting room in the ducal apartments, for it appeared two chambers led off to either side. Taken aback by the intimacy, she knew she must guard herself against this man's charm. How she wished things were different!

The Duke sat down across from her and placed his napkin in his lap. He smiled and acted as though this were something they did every morning.

She sat on the carved rosewood chair and watched him, waiting for him to speak. The waiting was worse than anything he could have to say, she decided.

"Please, help yourself," he offered.

He piled his plate high with sausages, coddled eggs and bacon. Then, holding a forkful before his mouth, he looked at her with the most endearing expression.

"Do you not wish to eat? Would you like something different? I can send to the kitchen." He frowned. "I suppose you know very well what I can send for. You did not prepare this, did you?"

She shook her head. "I do not think I can eat."

"Why ever not?" He placed his fork down with a reluctant gaze at the food.

"I fear what you will say to me."

"There is nothing to fear. I am afraid I cannot speak when I am hungry. Will you at least have a roll? Coffee? Tea?"

She reached out for a roll, realizing the dreaded conversation would only be delayed until he had had his fill.

They both took a few bites in silence and then he reached for her hand. His touch felt unlike any other. She stared at their joined fingers and when his thumb began to caress the back of her hand, she almost could not bear the mix of tenderness and longing she felt. He did not even seem to notice what he was doing!

"Meg, look at me," he commanded.

His gaze was intense, but did not fill her with revulsion as Thurgood's had—quite the opposite. He had wanted nothing but ownership of her. Luke's gaze held something more—desire, she thought, or perhaps affection was closer a description.

"Why did you think to escape again?" he asked softly. No, he was most definitely not like Thurgood, who would have bellowed his anger.

"Are you afraid of me?" he continued.

Meg wondered if it would help for her to lie to him, but she sensed it would hurt him deeply. "No, I am not afraid of you, but I do fear for you if you continue on the path you seem to be determined upon."

"It is my duty to protect you," he protested. There was a fierce look in his eyes. Had she offended him?

"My uncle would not hesitate to call you out and kill you," she elaborated. "He sold me to pay his gambling debts. Any man with so little conscience would not quibble over shooting a duke."

"I promise you, that will not happen without severe repercussions. I have already seen to it."

How could he be so confident? She was afraid to ask. Nibbling her lower lip pensively, she remained silent.

"I have sent for my mother, and you will remain here as her guest. She was friends with your mother and there has long been an understanding that we would join our esteemed families."

"There was?" Meg was astonished.

"As far as anyone else knows, yes. So, if your uncle protests—and he will not go against my word—he will face public ruin. It is very likely he will, anyway."

"I see... and if he stands down, you do realize that means we will have to wed?"

"Of course," he drawled in a bored manner.

"And what of Amelia? My presence here cannot be made known until she is safe. You cannot wed both of us!"

"I intend to invite her to stay with us."

Meg could not believe this man. He thought he could snap his fingers and she would marry him, her uncle would cease his evil ways, and he would release Amelia! "So our fate is sealed? I have no say?"

"Our fate was sealed from the moment we crossed paths in Portsmouth, my dear. At the very least, the moment you chose my roof for your protection."

She shook her head. The conceit of the man! "Only because of your sense of duty," she snapped. "I could walk away this moment and no one would know."

"Is marriage to me so repulsive? If you cannot bear the thought of being my Duchess when you reach your majority, you may release me from the betrothal."

He was very direct. "I did not say so, but we hardly know one another." She knew it was a poor excuse, and she was half in love with the man already.

"I know enough."

Mayhap he did, yet would it be enough for her?

CHAPTER 13

Luke was busy sorting through the business that Graham deemed urgent when the post arrived. Luke rose to see if anything had come from Waverley or Farringdon. He was growing anxious to have information that would help the case against Meg's uncle.

Graham was there before him accepting the missive from the butler, and Luke directed the secretary into his study.

"It appears we have word from the Runners," he remarked as he handed one of the letters over.

Luke sat behind his desk, broke open the seal and began scanning the rough penmanship.

THE VILLAGE FOLK here are hesitant to speak poorly against the new Marquess. It is clear they are afraid of him. The old Marquess and his family were greatly esteemed and are sorely missed. The people are suspicious, however, and have been more free with their tongues since Hawthorne left for Town. One has admitted to seeing the new Hawthorne's man around the time of the deaths, but no one can say for certain if they were there before.

As far as the boating accident is concerned, it is believed the fault was with the boat. There was no poor weather that day, but people seem satisfied that the sea is fickle enough for the explanation to be possible. The boat did wash up on the shore with a great hole in the hull.

I do not know that there is more to be found here, Humberside being remote and of small population. There is not enough evidence to convict but enough say it is possible. We will await your direction.

"Deuce take it," Luke muttered in frustration. He looked up to see Tobin and Graham waiting.

"Bad news?" Tobin asked.

"It neither convicts nor vindicates Hawthorne."

"Does it provide for the possibility?" Graham asked.

"Yes. We must find out when Major Blake and his batman left the Peninsula." He held out the letter and Tobin took it and began reading. "See if you discern something I do not."

Tobin frowned as he read the missive and then handed it on to Graham, who scanned furiously. Luke waited.

"I agree, your Grace. If you have proof he could have been there, and his man was seen, then you at least have room for negotiations."

"*Or threats,*" Luke corrected.

"Tobin, can you look into that on my behalf at the War Office? Graham will send a letter with you."

"As ye wish," he answered in a manner indicating he was anything but pleased.

"Well, if you prefer to greet my mother, I will go instead."

"Give her me best," Tobin saluted and muttered on his way out of the door. Tobin had never been fond of nobility, especially matrons. Luke chuckled as he heard the front door close behind his batman.

"Is there anything else urgent, Graham?"

"No, your Grace. I am afraid the jeweller had nothing of import to say about the locket, other than it appears French in origin, and returned it to me." He held out a small velvet pouch and Luke took it. Meg would be pleased to have it back, and it was an excellent excuse to check how she did.

"Now that we know who she is, it does not appear to have been necessary after all. If you have no further need of me...?"

"No, your Grace." He gathered his papers and left the room. Luke waited until he heard the secretary's office door close and then he began mounting the stairs to the family apartments. Graham would be scandalized if he knew Lady Margaret was here, unchaperoned, so Luke would not inform him until his mother arrived. He had a plan for proceeding in his mind, and it only needed his mother's approval. Until she arrived, he would see how Meg was faring. Hopefully, after a good night's sleep she would be well rested and comprehend that being his Duchess would be an excellent match and that she had nothing to fear on his behalf.

He knocked lightly on the door and heard no answer. Frowning, he looked around for a servant, but remembered he had told them to absent themselves from this corridor. Turning the handle gently, he opened the door and looked into the room, but saw no one.

"Meg?" he called, but there was still no answer. He pushed open the door to the pale lilac room, only to find it empty. Where could she have gone?

Immediately, Luke began to panic. Thoughts of Meg on the street, lying wounded or dead, flashed through his mind before it leapt to Thurgood's men finding her and sailing for America, taking Meg against her will. He ran down the stairs, seeing red, ready to march straight to Hawthorne's town house and strangle him with one hand for doing this to her.

He began to look in every room in case she had not run away, yet she had threatened to do it, and she had probably already been gone some time.

"Your sense of honour will be the death of me, woman!" he said, hurrying from room to room and causing the servants to stop and stare. He could not even ask any of them if they had seen her, for they did not know of her existence. Surely, Meg was causing him to lose his mind and they did not even have an understanding!

Where could she be? Tobin was gone, Graham did not know she was here, the only other person she might have confided in was Cook.

He stumbled in haste down the stairs to the kitchens. When he found her, he was going to throttle her before he kissed her soundly!

As he approached the kitchen, he heard sounds of laughter and halted in his tracks. He felt so relieved that he leaned his head against the wall and closed his eyes. She had not run away. He waited for his heart to settle down before he turned and walked back up to his study, trying not to dwell on what his reaction meant.

MEG WAS TRYING NOT to think about being held prisoner. She had noticed there were servants placed discreetly at every door and were likely outside the gates to the park. However, she had escaped down to the kitchens for tea in a small mark of defiance. The Duke would never know, but she did. Cook was her friend, and it felt almost normal to be down here. All the servants were in a bit of a flurry, preparing for Lady Laurence's arrival, so she sat at a table and tried to stay out of the way. Cook would not allow her to help, so she eventually made her way back to her new room, thinking to console herself with one of the books the Duke had thoughtfully provided. Sitting at the dressing table, she removed the glasses and mob-cap when she saw the familiar velvet pouch, with a note, on her dressing table.

I THOUGHT *you might like to have this back.*
   Waverley

MEG ALLOWED the locket to slip from the pouch and lovingly fingered the ruby and sapphire stones on the front as memories of her parents enveloped her. She closed her eyes and allowed some tears to fall. "What would you have me do?" she whispered to the heavens as she looked out of her new window which viewed the front drive and a park just beyond the front gates.

Most of her wanted to stay and take comfort in the Duke's shelter and power. He made it seem easy to rely upon him and trust him. He had almost convinced her that he held her in some affection.

Two carriages pulled up in front of the house and Meg had to shake herself back to the present. A footman handed a lady down from the crested conveyance and the Duke was there to greet her. Meg stared in a most impolite fashion but she was curious. It was difficult to see with the violet bonnet hiding her, but Lady Laurence carried herself with a grace which reminded Meg of her mother. Her heart felt heavy in her chest, and again she could only pray that Amelia was safe. Wishing for what could never be would be of no benefit to either of them.

A knock on the door recalled her to the present again and she walked across the room to open it. "Mrs. Simms," she greeted her visitor, thankful that the Duke had not seen her in the servants' costume again.

"Lady Laurence wishes for you to join her for tea," the housekeeper explained.

"So soon? She does not wish to rest?"

"I believe she wishes it to appear that you arrived with her." She leaned forward and whispered, "Shall I help you dress?"

Meg nodded to the housekeeper, while wondering what the Duke's mother must think of her. Could Lady Laurence be persuaded to help her escape? She must not wish for her son to be involved in what must surely become an awful scandal.

Mrs. Simms helped her to change, then led her past two doors to a sitting room which was similar to the one where she had breakfasted with the Duke the day before. This room was bright with canary-coloured draperies and upholstery, with a rose floral print on the papered walls. Expecting a verbal lashing, she looked up to greet the lady and prepared for the worst. Even though she had done nothing wrong, she did not expect her to be pleased with this turn of events. How much did she know already?

"Oh my dear," Lady Laurence surprised her by saying. "Come, let me have a look at you." She held her arms out and greeted her like a long lost friend.

Meg went closer to the lady and dropped into a respectful curtsy before clasping the hands held out to her.

"My lady, thank you for coming to assist me." A keen blue-eyed gaze, much like her son's fell upon Meg's face. She was a very handsome woman, and did not seem old enough to have a grown son.

"You look very much like Frances."

Astonishment must have crossed her face.

"You are surprised? Your mother and I were the closest of friends. We had our come out together." She waved her hand towards the wing-back chair opposite her and Meg sat down.

"Luke wrote to me of your unfortunate circumstances and I came as quickly as I could. While I would do it for anyone in your situation, I do have a personal interest in my friend's daughter."

"Did the Duke tell you about my sister?"

"Yes, and I am undecided as to how to handle that particular situation. Luke is trying to determine if she came to London with your uncle. I am of a mind to call on the Marquess myself and see."

"I do not feel easy about involving you or the Duke in this."

"Nonsense. Your mother would expect nothing less. I, myself, would have expected it of her were it my own daughter."

"I could leave here now and no one would be the wiser," Meg protested.

"Do you not wish to marry? You could do much worse than my son."

"You misunderstand me. I do not wish to force him into an arranged marriage or place him in danger from my uncle."

"I was under the impression you were fond of each other," the lady said, frowning.

"He is merely being gallant and has resigned himself to the notion we must marry since I have been under his roof. It was no fault of his own, I assure you."

"It was our wish when you were children that our families would one day unite," she stated. "We made no formal arrangements, however, for we are not so old-fashioned."

"You are not saying that for my conscience?" Meg questioned.

"Not at all, my dear. Does it help to know?" She smiled knowingly.

"A little," Meg confessed. "I was hoping you would be on my side and help me move to another location. I do not think it will be easy for me to hide until my majority, nor to find a way to help my sister escape my uncle's plans."

"I have no intention of helping you do something so foolish. We must face this head on and if, in the end, you become a duchess, there are worse fates, like 'Mrs. Thurgood'."

Meg sighed. The lady was well informed. It would be much easier to have help; besides the obvious difficulties of breaking in and abducting Amelia, she had no money and nowhere else to go. "What do you propose we do?"

"We present you as Luke's betrothed as intended by our families when you were children. You will go to small Society events by my side as appropriate for your state of mourning."

"You mean to let my uncle know I am here? To flaunt my defiance in his face?" She shook her head. "I cannot jeopardize Amelia in such a way. He will take his wrath out on her."

"It is a game we must play. He is very conscious of his station and by placing you under Luke's protection, he would be calling us liars."

"But what of Mr. Thurgood? He paid my uncle an exorbitant sum of money for me."

"And your uncle arranged that in an underhanded fashion to pay off debts, I assume? You are still in mourning and he took you from your home, in the dead of night, without seeing you married first. He will not want that made known publicly. How would he have explained your absence? I assume he would have said you had eloped."

"Quite possibly."

"As we speak, there have been no rumours concerning you or your sister, so we still have the upper hand."

"I pray you are correct," Meg said, unconvinced it would be as easy as she thought.

"Now, we must procure some appropriate clothing for you since you have none. I presume?"

"This is what I was wearing when I jumped from the ship," Meg confirmed.

"It is in surprisingly good condition," her ladyship remarked.

"I have been fortunate in my rescuers and those who have helped me along the way."

"You have angels looking after you from above," she said kindly as she took Meg's hand. "I know I am not your mother, but I do think you and my son are well suited. You may take comfort in knowing your parents would be pleased with the match."

Meg felt her throat burning with emotion. It was difficult to think of her recent loss without bursting into tears, but she did not have the luxury of mourning properly. She must be strong for herself and her sister. Although marrying Luke would be a luxury in any situation, she vowed she would not hold him to the marriage if there was not genuine affection on both their parts when this horrid ordeal was over.

CHAPTER 14

*L*uke very much wished he had one of his brothers in arms present to pay this call, but he settled for his secretary to accompany him. He was not such a fool as to go alone. While not expecting a scene at a hotel such as Grillon's, one never knew what to expect from new money and an individual who had not been raised as a gentleman.

They arrived at the hotel with the pomp and circumstance due to a duke, hoping to impress upon the cit that in England he must deal with Luke as Waverley. He had heard that American money was impressed by titles, and he could only hope it was the case with Mr. Thurgood.

Mr. Graham presented Luke's card to the hotel concierge and he was immediately told to proceed to his suite of rooms. As they climbed the stairs, Luke was dreading this meeting, but he deemed it necessary to join forces with this man. He could not fight both him and Hawthorne at the same time. Perhaps he should have invited him to meet elsewhere, but he did not want the man at his house, and preferred the element of surprise.

Luke waited while his secretary knocked on the door and presented his card again.

The servant did not mask his surprise when he read the card. "Please do come in and I will let Mr. Thurgood know you are here." He showed them into a handsome sitting room overlooking Albermarle Street. The chamber was dressed in luxurious velvet green draperies with paintings to rival those found in most noble houses. "Please make yourself comfortable. May I offer you refreshment?"

"No, thank you." The servant at least had manners, Luke mused. His first impressions of Thurgood had not been as good.

Luke stood watching the bustling pedestrian traffic along the crowded street surrounded by four-storey brick and stone buildings on all sides. A few carriages made their way through, their horses hooves resounding on the cobblestones.

A few minutes later, the man himself burst into the room. "I remember you," he boomed. "You did not say you were a duke."

"It was not important at the time," Luke drawled.

"Have you news of my betrothed?"

"I have, in fact. I regret to inform you, however, that she is not yours."

Thurgood's face took on a deep purple hue, much as Luke had expected. He would like nothing more than to plant him a facer, but it would not serve his purpose...yet. First, however, he needed to find out what the man knew. He held up a hand.

"I have not come as an enemy," Luke began.

The man looked wary.

"It has come to my attention that Hawthorne has tried to dupe you—us."

"Go on." The man crossed his arms over his chest, which rested on his ample stomach.

"You did not give me the name of your betrothed when we chanced to meet in Portsmouth."

"I do not suppose I did," he replied. "I was distraught over her sudden disappearance."

"Since that time, it has come to my attention that Hawthorne has played you for a fool. Lady Margaret was already promised to me when he sold her."

"Now listen here, I did not buy her like a slave!" His arms had come down to his sides, and his fists were balled.

"Did she agree to marry you, willingly?" Luke taunted.

"According to Hawthorne, she did. He brought her to my ship, saying she felt poorly and how was I to know any different? We were to wed in Massachusetts at my family home, being respectful to her parents' passing. The next thing I knew, she was missing."

"I see," Luke said, hoping to sound sympathetic. He could see how the arrangement had taken place. "It seems we have both been played false."

"I just want her back."

"But she is not willing and is promised to me. Have you told Hawthorne she went missing?"

"Aye. I sent a note straight away, demanding to know what happened! He says she did not return to the Abbey, and it was not his fault I did not keep her safe." He pouted, which was so very unbecoming on a grown man.

Luke stood and walked toward the window, hands clasped behind his back, debating how much to reveal. "No, she came to me."

"I demand satisfaction!" the American roared.

Luke turned his head slightly, giving the man a bored look. "I assumed as much. It is why I am here. I suggest we join forces to see Hawthorne brought to justice."

Luke waited while Thurgood thought over this information. Many emotions seemed to cross his expressive face, from anger to resignation to revenge.

"What do you have in mind? I want my money back if I cannot have the girl."

"Quite understandable. Do you agree to cease your attentions towards Lady Margaret?"

"If she is already promised to you, then I understand why she ran away. Why did she not just say so?"

"That is very good of you," Luke said dryly, though Thurgood seemed unaware of the sarcasm. "I imagine her uncle left her no choice in the matter."

"I will call on him now and demand repayment," the man said in a decisive manner as he hurried to the door.

"May I ask a small favour of you?"

The man halted and turned around.

"Do not tell him where she is, yet. I wish to ensure her sister's safety first."

Thurgood shrugged. "It makes no difference to me, so long as you return the favour when needed."

Luke held out his hand in agreement. The man looked pleased as he squeezed it with force. Luke hoped he would not come to regret this one day, but the man seemed harmless enough when faced with the truth; his major offence being vulgarity.

They left the chamber together and were followed by several servants as they proceeded downstairs. Collecting their hats and gloves from the doorman, Luke, his escort and Thurgood waited in a group for their carriages to be brought around.

"By the by, how did you become involved with Hawthorne?" Luke asked.

"Business, as is the usual way for the aristocracy. They snub us until they need our money."

"I was not aware Hawthorne was involved in trade."

"The new Marquess most certainly is. I first met him three years ago in a card game. He traded his vowels to get me an army contract," the man confided smugly.

Thurgood's carriage arrived and called him away before Luke could enquire further... and Luke stood watching, feeling his jaw clench.

"THE MAJOR WILL HAVE my hide if he hears of this," Tobin growled.

"Then we must make sure he does not hear," Meg replied as she placed her thick glasses on her nose to complete her disguise, having pulled her dark hat low.

"I don't think this will work."

"You have made that clear, but I must try to do something."

"I should not have told you she was here," he opined as she saw him check his dagger in his boot and his pistol in his waistband.

"You did the right thing. I will make certain the Duke understands I gave you little choice in the matter, if it comes to that."

"I feel ever so comforted. What if yer uncle spies ye and captures ye?"

"He will not think me anything other than the servant I appear to be."

Tobin scanned her groom's trousers with a muttered curse, as she relished the freedom provided. He was still shaking his head when he rapped on the ceiling of the carriage and they alighted a street away from Hawthorne House. It was dark and the wind was biting, even through the thick coat and gloves she wore. With Meg following Tobin, they crept like criminals around the back of the house, and she slid her glasses down low on her nose so she could see.

The house was of large gold, rectangular stones and three storeys tall, but slightly narrower than Waverley Place. A garden lay between the house and the mews, and Tobin looked around before trying the iron gate. He made quick work of the lock with some type of metal tool he had brought, and they hurried inside, closing it quickly behind them. Tobin guided her forward to a terrace, where lights shone through the windows.

Trembling with a gnawing fear of discovery, she forced herself forward, knowing this must be done. A staying hand held her back as two grooms walked along the path from the house to the stables talking jovially with one another. She had been so lost in her thoughts she had not noticed them. When they were out of sight, Tobin motioned for her to follow him as he moved towards a window. Having never been in London, Meg was unfamiliar with the house. Sitting less than five feet in front of the window, with his back to her, was her uncle. She smothered a gasp as she saw Amelia across the table from him dining on their supper.

"She looks well," Meg whispered with relief as she stared lovingly at the familiar copper locks and bright eyes of her sibling.

"Aye," Tobin agreed, looking dumbstruck. Meg would have laughed in any other circumstances, but she had to find a way to get a message to her sister. Fingering the letter in her pocket, she stepped back to survey the house.

"If only I knew which room was hers."

"Faith, me lady, ye are not climbing up the side of the house!" he commanded under his breath.

"I most certainly am. How else am I to leave the letter for my sister?"

"Heaven help me to keep from strangling me master's lady," he muttered loud enough for her to hear.

"Tobin, turn around and stand guard for me, please," she said in the sweetest voice she could muster.

"I did not know scaling walls was taught in finishin' school," he retorted.

"Ladies are full of surprises. Now, give me a boost up," she ordered.

Ignoring her while reverting to Gaelic for his rantings, he began climbing the wall before she knew what he was about. She stared, gazing upwards while at the same time trying to listen for any sounds of guards or servants close by, but she was worried he would fall. The ledge above was small and now she felt guilty for having forced him into this start.

Realizing she still had the letter, she tried to follow around the house as he looked in each window. Tobin disappeared around the side of the house, and she grew impatient as she waited, not being able to exit the garden. Dancing in place in a vain attempt to stay warm, she almost screamed when his face appeared upside down before her. She jumped and gasped and was certain she must have been heard by someone other than her cohort.

"Quickly, I need the letter!" he commanded.

"Did you find her room?"

"I believe so," he replied as he held his hand down.

"Let us pray you are correct. It is a great risk we are taking," she reminded him as she handed over the folded letter.

"It is a bit late for a lecture!" he chided as he pulled himself back upright on the ledge.

"Leave it inside the second drawer of her jewellery box. We always place our lockets there ourselves at night."

"I will do me best." Then he disappeared.

She dared to walk back to the window and try to steal one last glance at her sister and reaffirm that she was well, but when she looked into the dining room, no one was there. She scurried to the next window, but the drawing room was empty. She began to panic and went back to where she left Tobin.

Whispering wildly, she tried to get his attention, but then heard sounds of alarm coming from one of the rooms above, as a door crashed and a window opened with a bang.

A scream of "thief!" sounded, followed by the frantic sounds of Tobin trying to escape. A body fell into the nearby brushes with a yelp of pain.

Tobin jumped up quickly and grabbed her arm, forcing her to run with him as he hurried for the gate as fast as her legs could go. The sounds of the household stirring to come after this intruder were evident as doors banged, voices shouted calls for help, a dog barked its displeasure, and noises and footsteps followed their retreat down the alley. Meg's heart pounded loudly in her chest as they ran for the carriage as fast as possible, thankful she was not wearing skirts. Tobin shoved her into the waiting carriage and hopped in as the horses lurched into their collars.

Breathing heavily, neither one of them could speak as they tried to come down from their adventure. Tobin stood awkwardly instead of sitting.

"Are you harmed?"

"*Níl aon tóin tinn mar do thóin tinn féin,*" he snapped.

"Oh dear. On our return I will send for the doctor." She understood his intoned meaning, anyway.

"I do not need a sawbones," he growled. "I landed on a rosebush is all."

Meg did not know what to say. Her tally of guilt was growing by leaps and bounds.

"I will help you, then."

"It would not be proper. I will have the Major help me. We have been through worse before."

"And risk him knowing what we have done? I think not!" she protested.

"Now she has a care for my well-being," he muttered to the roof of the conveyance.

She folded her arms across her chest, at once in a huff. "Did you at least deliver the letter?"

"I did. I was on my way back out of the door when her maid came inside. I hope they do not search everythin', thinkin' tha' I was a thief. I did not disturb anythin'."

"Hopefully they will not do so before Amelia discovers my letter. I do not know what she must think has happened to me by now."

"It is in the Lord's hands now," he said with surprising kindness.

"I suppose so, but it is hard to sit idle, waiting to discover our fate."

The carriage pulled in behind the mews and they returned to the house as quietly as they could, sneaking up the servants stairs to her sitting room after seeking nursing supplies from Cook.

Meg ordered Tobin face down on a sofa in the sitting room, and began extracting thorns from his backside with as much propriety as could be had in such a situation.

"I feel terrible," Meg apologized. "You should have let me climb the wall."

"Dinna fash yerself," he said dismissively. "'Tis nothin' but a few scratches."

"What is the meaning of this?" an angry voice boomed from the doorway.

CHAPTER 15

Never before had Luke thought himself prone to the base emotion of jealousy, but when he saw his future wife bending over the body of his batman and speaking to him in casual terms, he burned with the emotion.

"Luke!" Meg looked up at him, surprise and guilt evident in her beautiful eyes. She was wearing the outfit of one of his grooms and it was all he could do not to devour her slender frame, so clearly revealed, with his own gaze. With difficulty, he pulled his eyes to her face. She waved her arms over his man for explanation. "Tobin fell into a thorny bush."

Luke leaned casually against the door frame. "And you had to dress like that and help him yourself?"

"It seemed the least intrusive course to your household," she explained. As he watched, her cheeks took on a rosy hue.

Luke knew he would never be able to stay angry with this woman. She had cast a spell over him! Tobin, on the other hand, was grinning broadly while trying to hide his face in his arms.

"Mr. O'Neill, would you like to make some sense of the situation in terms that I will understand?"

"No, yer Grace. I think Lady Meg is doing perfectly well by herself.

Ouch!" he exclaimed as she pulled a large thorn from his backside then carefully moving the cloths from place to place over his behind to keep him covered.

Luke had to smother laughter. Whatever they had become mixed up in, Tobin was serving his penance. Luke took a seat in a nearby armchair and crossed his legs to watch the show. "Shall I send for the doctor?"

"I am almost finished, thank you," she snapped haughtily.

"Excellent, because I am enjoying the spectacle very much. Shall I ring for refreshment instead? I cannot wait to hear the story."

"I should appreciate a dram of whiskey," Tobin remarked with a mischievous twinkle in his eye.

Luke reached over and tugged on the bell-pull. He intercepted the tray himself when it arrived so no servants would be tempted to gossip about what they had seen. Meg had finished with Tobin and was taking a very long time dressing the wounds and cleaning up her tools, he noticed. "Please have a seat."

She took the high-back chair furthest away from him and stared at her hands. He poured her a small amount of whisky and handed it to her, deliberately holding her fingers over the glass until she looked up at him.

Tobin cleared his throat, but Luke ignored the reminder. He would deal with him later.

"Would you please tell me where Tobin fell into this bush? Although I have no doubt I can wring the truth from him, I would much prefer to hear it in your words." He cast a sideways glare at his batman. Let her think his threat was not idle. He could get the story from Tobin if necessary.

"You promise you will not harm Tobin?" she asked, her tone full of uncertainty.

Luke continued to glare at Tobin, but the insolent servant smiled.

"I promise not to kill him," Luke clarified.

Meg was looking at her glass so she missed the look which passed between the two men.

"I forced him to go with me. Please do not be angry." She swallowed loudly. "We went to Hawthorne's house to see if we could set eyes on my sister."

"And did you?" He was astonished. How could they have been so stupid?

She nodded. "She was dining with my uncle."

He waited but Meg offered nothing further. He was going to have to prod the information from her.

"Is that all? I assume this was done clandestinely?"

"Yes. We entered through the back garden and looked in from the window. I was going to climb to my sister's room, but Tobin went."

It was clear she was trying to confess as little as possible, yet he had a feeling there was more to it.

"And how did Tobin come by the thorns? I know my batman very well, and he appreciates his... ah, posterior... very much. He would not have stumbled upon them by accident."

"Thank ye, yer Grace," Tobin added with heavy sarcasm.

"He fell, your Grace."

"And how did you fall?" He directed this question at Tobin.

"A maid came into the room so I had to hurry."

"Naturally. Were you discovered?"

"Possibly." Tobin shrugged in his off-handed Irish way.

"Do you know or not?" Luke tried not to growl.

"'Twas a bit of a commotion upon me exit. We might have proceeded with haste to the waitin' carriage."

Luke could not believe what he was hearing. He leaned forward and dropped his head into his hands, which were resting on his knees. It would do no good to yell at this point. What was done was done.

"So now we must see if the letter is discovered. How do you expect her to communicate with you? The letter was delivered, I trust?"

"Saints above!" Tobin buried his face in his arms.

"The milkmaid agreed to help us," Meg answered, "if Amelia can get a letter to her."

Luke looked from one to the other.

"Most ladies are not immune to my charms," Tobin shrugged, clearly enjoying every minute.

"I also had a productive evening," Luke remarked.

Both Meg and Tobin looked up expectantly. He took a long sip of his whisky, prolonging the suspense. "I went to see Thurgood."

Meg leaned forward, waiting.

"He claims your uncle assured him you were willing to marry him. Hawthorne told him you were feeling unwell and took you straight to your cabin. It did not occur to him to think otherwise, and the wedding was to take place in America."

"Was anyone there to chaperone me? Of course not, the scoundrel! Anyone who would drug an innocent to force her on to a boat has no conscience."

"I do not know if Thurgood understands the niceties of Polite Society, but your uncle certainly would. He meant to be assured you could not return unmarried."

"Is Thurgood still determined to find me?" Concern was evident on her face. Luke wanted to reach over and wipe away the furrow between her brows.

"I do not believe so. I did my best to refocus his ire on Hawthorne. I told him you ran away because we were already promised to one another. He feels very ill-used and wants his money back."

"I do not think my uncle has it. What will happen when Thurgood discovers that?"

"I cannot say." Although, he would not put it past Hawthorne to offer for Amelia instead, but he would not voice that. Hawthorne would certainly try to save his own skin.

MEG WAS RELIEVED to escape the room. Luke had been very understanding of their escapade. It had been an exceedingly close thing, however, and she would have to be more cautious next time. Next time? Shaking her head at her wandering thoughts, she opened the door to her chamber to find Cook's niece, Susie, waiting for her. The girl stood up and dropped a curtsy.

"I am to be your maid while you are here, my lady, if it pleases you."

"It pleases me very much, Susie. I have no other gowns to wear apart from the lavender from yesterday, so if you will help me to don the muslin again, it will have to do for tonight." Meg walked to her dressing table and began to dispose of some outer garments.

"Lady Laurence sent up a gown for you, my lady."

Meg turned back to the maid in surprise. "However did she find one so quickly?"

"I believe it belongs to his Grace's sister. She is at school in Bath," the maid explained as she took the jackets and trousers from Meg with nary a remark about her unconventional costume.

The maid knew far more than she did about the Duke's family, apparently. Susie went into the dressing room and Meg followed. Hanging there was a simple black silk gown that would suit very well. She must remember to thank Lady Laurence. After dressing, she joined the Duke and his mother downstairs.

After the past week, sitting to the Duke's table seemed a ridiculous luxury. It should be easy to fall back into her world, but did she want to? The three of them were alone, *en famille*, and Meg remained quiet as they chatted about family matters. This was the first his mother had seen of him since his return from the Peninsular War.

Her thoughts were interrupted by Lady Laurence as bowls of turtle soup were placed before them.

"Lady Margaret, forgive us for boring you with things of which you have no interest." She smiled. "I have sent notices to the papers, announcing the betrothal and stating the proceedings will take place quietly, but as planned by our families, before the unexpected passing of your parents."

Meg was shocked. She supposed she should not be, they had stated their intentions, but she had not expected a public announcement. What would this do to Amelia's situation?

"Forgive me, my lady, but what of my sister? I believe we should have waited until she was safe."

"My dear, I understand your feelings, but this will help her cause.

Should your uncle try to secretly wed her to the old Earl, there will be an outcry. I intend to hold a betrothal dinner where she may be presented to the pillars of the *ton*. If she has your beauty, it will be impossible for Hawthorne to hide her away."

Meg placed her spoon down beside her plate. She felt sick about all of it. She did not wish to play games with her uncle.

"Besides, she has the potential to make a more advantageous match than Lord Erskine. I hope to take her under my wing and convince your uncle of that."

"It is likely there are more devious reasons he has agreed to a match in that quarter," the Duke interjected. From the tilt of his head it was clear he had been quietly listening. "He is her guardian and there is little I can do to gainsay him on the subject of Lady Amelia."

"He will not appreciate attempts at interference," Meg agreed. "I shudder to think what his reaction will be when he finds out I am here."

"You are not to leave my side until this is resolved," he commanded with a direct look.

She wanted to be angered, but the look held concern, and it felt good to have someone care. Her cheeks began to heat under his stare, and she wished his mother was not there to witness the look.

Lady Laurence cleared her throat and pretended great interest in the fruit before her. The awkward moment passed and thankfully, the rest of the dinner was more mundane. Lady Laurence kept the talk light-hearted, introducing the topic of the antics engaged in by Julia and her friends from school. When the lady finally rose, signalling the end of dinner, Luke also stood.

"Mother, do you think Lady Margaret and I might have a word alone?"

She raised her brows a little at this but nodded her acquiescence. "I am not yet accustomed to city hours, and you are betrothed. I will retire now," she said with a look that indicated he should not forget his place. Meg found this humorous, since any number of things could have happened before her arrival, but she kept silent. She also noticed a reciprocating twinkle in Luke's eye as he came to stand before her and held out his arm. He walked her into a small study at the back of the house. A roaring fire sat to one side of the room flanked by two comfortably worn leather armchairs. A sofa sat in front of a wall of books, which looked out through glass doors onto the terrace. Leading her to one of the chairs, he sat down opposite her. It was very quaint and domestic; it would be very easy to forget why she was here.

"Should I call for tea?"

"Not for me," she said with a slight pat to her stomach. "You have the most excellent chef," she teased.

"To think, a few days ago, I did not know who was baking my bread."

"I consider it a compliment if you did not detect a difference," she replied with her chin in the air.

He laughed and reached over, holding out his hand. "May I?"

"I— I suppose so." She tentatively placed her hand in his.

"We are to be married. I thought we should spend more time becoming acquainted." The warm look in his eyes heated her more effectively than the nearby fire.

"Your Grace..." She began to protest.

"Luke," he corrected. "I know you are concerned for your sister, but there is nothing further we can do tonight. We have set the wheels in motion as best we can, and now we must wait."

She relaxed a bit as his fingers began tenderly caressing her hand again, sending sensations straight to her insides. They had not replaced their gloves after dinner, and she found the touch disconcerting yet also soothing.

"Luke, I was objecting to the need to tie yourself to me in matrimony. Somehow, it seems you have managed to protect my reputation, thus far," she said, though disjointedly, having difficulty forming the words when the two of them were so intimately situated.

"Am I so objectionable, Meg? Look at me," he commanded gently.

She did and suddenly she was drowning. The light of the fire accentuated his masculine beauty in such a way she felt she must be in a dream, except his presence, his scent clouded her senses and overtook her good judgement.

Had he asked her a question? Indeed he had. Objectionable? "No," she whispered. "Nevertheless, it does not mean it is wise." Her heart and her head battled for her attention.

"May I at least have the opportunity to change your mind?"

Before it occurred to her to object, a hand came up to cradle her face and his thumb gently brushed against her lower lip. She let out a nervous breath as his lips descended to brush lightly over hers then more firmly, touching, feeling, tasting. It was an entirely new sensation and so strangely intimate, yet not at all repulsive as she would have thought. Somehow her hands found their way around his neck and she was returning his kiss with abandon until his lips left hers and he pulled her into an embrace while chuckling. He was amused? Her wits had completely gone begging and he was laughing?

"I do not think I can survive any more convincing tonight," he murmured, his lips against her hair. Well, at least one of them had their wits about them.

CHAPTER 16

*L*uke was having great difficulty in concentrating on his solicitor's words the next morning. He tried to drag his mind away from kissing Meg the night before, but the more he endeavoured not to think about it, the more he thought about it.

"Your Grace? Should I perhaps arrange this discussion for another time? You seem a bit preoccupied," the portly old gentleman asked as he stroked his white whiskers.

"My apologies, Mr. Ramsey. I am preoccupied, but it is no fault of yours. The settlements need to be done. Please continue." He sat up taller at his desk and tried to focus his mind on the task before him.

The solicitor cleared his throat and sat up taller as he stacked some papers together. "When I attempted to make an appointment with the previous Marquess's solicitor, I received a note in response to say he was no longer serving the family." Mr. Ramsey leaned forward and smacked his hand on the table. "They had been serving the family for six generations!" His face showed signs of horror. "Six!"

Luke leaned forward reassuringly. "The House of Waverley has no intention of dismissing Ramsey and Sons."

The solicitor nodded, apparently too upset to speak. He composed himself and then cleared his throat and began again, sitting taller and stacking his papers. It must be his preparatory ritual, Luke decided.

"As I was saying, the new Marquess has taken on a new solicitor." He paused to frown again, apparently unable to fathom such a distasteful action. "I was referred to a new office, of which I had never heard before—a Mr. Percival Jones. I have been unable to gain an audience yet. I did, however, receive a copy of the previous Hawthorne's will. Lady Margaret's portion, due upon her marriage or her majority, includes twenty-five thousand pounds and an estate in Essex. Two widowed ladies are currently residing there as pensioners. I have drawn up the settlements with the assumption this has not changed."

"Does Lady Amelia have a similar marriage portion?"

"I would expect so, your Grace. I did not read about the sister."

"I would not rely on any of this being available. I believe the new Hawthorne intends to keep everything for himself. I am pleased you have copies of all the documents. They may be needed in the future to remove his guardianship of the Lady Amelia."

Mr. Ramsey looked shocked. "Is this the new Marquess a thief?" he whispered.

"Quite possibly," Luke replied. "I have Runners investigating the death of Lady Margaret's parents. I am expecting more news any day, from the Peninsula, regarding the then Major Blake's movements prior to their death."

"Mercy," the solicitor gasped. "May I have your permission to alert the old firm of possible wrong-doing? Discreetly, of course, but sometimes there are suspicious behaviours..."

"At this point, I will be glad of anything to help Lady Margaret and Lady Amelia's plight. I fear it will not be good. If I had not found her when I did..." Luke had to swallow emotion and did not finish.

"I will prepare another copy of the settlements without her bringing a marriage portion, in that case." The solicitor seemed to understand.

"She will have use of the dower house until her death, of course, but I would also like her to have property in her own right. I think the estate in Lincolnshire, on the sea, would be nice for her. It is close to where she grew up."

"Yes, of course, your Grace." The solicitor scribbled a note to himself.

"The rest can remain as it is." Luke stood up so the solicitor could be on his way. As he was being shown out, someone else was arriving. Luke was not in the mood to see anyone just now. Speaking of Hawthorne had that effect on him. This needed to be resolved quickly. Perhaps, he mused hopefully, the caller was for his mother. As the butler knocked on the door, Luke sighed. "Come in, Timmons. I am not home for the rest of the day."

"Yes, your Grace, but this...gentleman insisted I at least show you his card." Luke took it from the silver salver on which it rested.

"Philip," he whispered. "Yes, show him up." What was Philip doing here?

He walked around his desk, pondering, when Philip's handsome dark face appeared at the door. They greeted one another with brotherly hugs and pats on the back.

Luke pulled on the bell-rope to request proper refreshment. "Shall I have a room prepared for you? How long are you here?"

"I do not know yet. I have business to attend to. I can stay at the club," Philip said dismissively.

"I would not hear of it." When a footman appeared at the door, Luke instructed him to bring up a proper breakfast and prepare a room for Captain Elliot. Luke sat down; Philip removed his sword and scabbard before also sitting.

"Coffee?" Luke asked, knowing that all of the brothers shared his vice in the morning. He refreshed his cup and then poured another for Philip before handing it to him. "Now, tell me what has brought you this way. It is a pleasant surprise, but a surprise nonetheless."

Philip crossed his legs and took a sip of coffee with an appreciative sigh. "When I showed Lord Wellington your note, he insisted I come to you at once."

Luke was stunned. "There must be a great deal of which I am unaware."

"Let us say that the plundering at Vitoria was a mild incident and the timing fortuitous. Wellington could not send him home fast enough."

"Gambling debts or worse?"

"He is a bad egg from every angle. Why the interest?" He placed his cup on the nearby table.

Luke grew quiet as he tried to think how best to word his queries. There was no delicate way to broach it, however.

"I wrote to you of his acquiring the title."

Philip nodded. "Quite a convenient coincidence," he added dryly.

"I am betrothed to his niece, whom he had drugged and sold to an American merchant. She awoke on a ship about to set sail, and jumped overboard to escape."

Philip slapped both of his hands down on the arms of the chair. "I knew Wellington should not have let him off so easily." He shook his head. "We had more than enough evidence to try him for his crimes when he was not a peer."

"'Tis why I am trying to gather proof that Lady Margaret's parents did not die by accident. I need to know precisely when Major Blake left the Peninsula. His man was seen in the vicinity around the time of the ship wreck, but I need to leave nothing to chance if I am to bring him before the Lords."

"You wish to drag her family's name through the public disgrace?" Philip frowned.

"Of course not," Luke countered. "But I need to be prepared to. I have an audience with Prinny and wish to state my suspicions with as many facts as possible."

"I can have that information quickly. It is in a log at the War Office. I want to verify the date, but I recall it being the twenty-second of June on an invalid ship."

"Wellington did not waste time. Thus far, my Runners have not been able to find any proof, only suspicion. The dates were not readily available when I sent Tobin to enquire."

Philip cursed. "Wellington will never forgive himself for allowing this to happen. He probably suspects as much, which is why he sent me personally. You have never mentioned you were betrothed," Philip remarked with a knowing look.

Luke waved his hand dismissively. "It was more of a cradle wish of our parents." It was not that he could not be truthful with Philip, whom he trusted with his life, but the least said to tarnish Meg's reputation, the better. He did not wish to explain his hasty betrothal—or obsession—to anyone.

"So, where is this fair maiden? If she escaped an imprisonment, I would not think she would have run back to her uncle."

Philip was very sharp... It was why he ran covert missions for Wellington.

"She is here, along with my mother," Luke added before Philip could speculate.

"Does Major Blake, ah, Hawthorne, know she is here?"

Luke picked up the morning paper and handed it to Philip. "He will know soon, if he does not already."

"What game are you playing?" Philip's eyes looked up from the announcement to search his.

"My mother thinks she will be safer if she is under my protection publicly. Meg, however, is worried about her sister, who is still with Blake. She says he plans to wed her to Erskine when they are out of mourning."

"I presume he will receive large sums of cash for her as well? The Hawthorne estate is one of the wealthiest in the country. I cannot imagine what he intends to do with it. It will fall to ruin quickly in his hands. He only had temporary command of the 18th, and you see how he managed that affair."

"I have had my man enquiring into Hawthorne's death. Blake covers his tracks well."

"I am not certain gambling is the extent of it," Philip said hesitantly.

Luke raised his brows but waited for Philip to finish.

"We suspect he was selling information. He was certainly accepting favours for positions amongst the battalion, and you know Peter's death was likely an ambush."

"A traitor to add to his sins," Luke said softly, although he was not in the least surprised. Thankfully Tobin's shame was unknown to others, but Luke hoped to save Meg from sharing her uncle's disgrace.

❧

MEG AWOKE EARLY the next morning, dressed herself, and hurried downstairs to wait in the kitchen. Cook raised her eyebrows at Meg's return to the servant's quarters but smiled and winked at her anyway.

"She is not back, yet," Cook answered the question before Meg could ask.

"Has she been gone long?"

"About half an hour. I expect her any minute." Cook continued her tasks while Meg toyed with a piece of dough she had pinched off an unbaked loaf. She dare not try to do anything resembling work for fear of a tongue-lashing.

Just then, the door opened and Susie came inside and shook off the chill from her limbs. She hung her cloak on a hook and walked over to the fire, holding out her hands to warm them. She had not noticed Meg sitting there at the work table.

"Well, have you any news?" Cook asked. "Lady Margaret is a-waiting."

Susie looked over and embarrassment shone on her face as she dropped a curtsy. "Forgive me, my lady."

Meg waved her hand dismissively. "Good morning, Susie. Did you find any news of my sister?"

"I did, my lady." She walked over to the cloak on the wall and pulling out a letter, handed it to Meg.

She nearly tore it with her anxiousness to read its contents. It was folded into a small square and sealed.

DEAREST MEG!

. . .

You cannot know my emotions upon seeing your letter. It was a very near thing that I discovered it before Uncle did. I suppose it was your servant who broke into my room to deliver it and was almost discovered. I am rambling, but my nerves are shattered. Would you believe that Uncle told me you had eloped with the awful Mr. Thurgood, without so much as a note telling me you were leaving? Naturally, I was distraught to discover his true character, but he has been very kind. Imagine my surprise when I read your letter! I did wonder at the haste with which we repaired to London, and now I wonder how I will pretend ignorance to Uncle's face. Please say you will discover a way to remove me from his presence as quickly as possible! I am permitted a walk in the park every afternoon before tea with my maid. Perhaps you can arrange to have someone slip me a note then.

Until then I will remain in uneasy ignorance and ever your devoted sister,

AMELIA

MEG DROPPED the paper on the table before her. It was a relief to know Uncle was treating her well. Of course, Amelia never gave anyone any trouble. However, she was not good at hiding her feelings and she hoped her uncle would not suspect anything now. It had been necessary to warn Amelia because she did not know how or when it may become required to act. Now her hand had been forced, and therefore her uncle's, and she feared the next scene in the play with all her heart. There were more actors involved now and she could not bear the thought of losing anyone else.

"Are you going to make us wait all day?" Cook asked impatiently.

Meg smiled. "It says very little. My sister did not know of my uncle's duplicity. He told her I had eloped without so much as a bye your leave!"

"The cur!"

"Yes. She did say she is permitted to walk in the park with a maid in the afternoons."

"Well, that is something, then. Lady Laurence is planning a dinner," she stated.

"Yes, she placed a betrothal notice in the papers this morning, with a dinner party to follow. I expect my uncle will do something soon."

"Maybe he will wait until the dinner. She mentioned she had invited him and your sister."

"I suppose I should discuss things further with the Duke. We should have a plan. Has he breakfasted yet?"

"He just requested it and I sent it up. I think he has company."

"So early?" Meg questioned.

"He was never an idle fellow before the military." Cook returned to her tasks and Meg left the kitchen wondering if she would be bothering Luke and his guest. Taking the path through the main entrance hall instead of using the servants' entrance, to which she had become accustomed, she decided it might embarrass Luke. She could not imagine who would be calling so early, but admitted to herself she really did not know much about him. As she walked, she heard the sounds of laughter and camaraderie echoing through the house. A footman stood ready to open the door, and for a moment she debated returning to her room and requesting a tray. Determining to have more confidence, she decided she would simply leave quickly if she was disturbing them. With a quick nod to the servant, she moved through the open door as he held it for her.

Pausing at the scene before her, she found the Duke smiling and another, darkly handsome, soldier looking much like the Duke had that first night when still in uniform. The sight of Luke thus was devastating. She began to recoil. "I beg your pardon. I did not mean to interrupt."

"Meg, wait!"

Both men had risen to their feet. "Lady Margaret Blake, may I present to you Captain Philip Elliot of the Guards and one of my dearest friends. In fact, we consider one another as brothers."

Captain Elliot took her hand and kissed the air above it. His dark eyes bored into hers. He positively oozed charm.

"*Enchanté*, Lady Margaret. If it is not too late, I cannot offer you the life of a duchess, but it will not be dull to follow the drum, none-theless."

Meg laughed, but did not know what to say.

"You are embarrassing her, Philip. Pay him no mind, Meg. Soldiers lose their sense of manners and decency when they see a beautiful woman. He is just off the ship. Please join us; he was bringing me up to speed on events over breakfast."

"I think I would be *de trop*. I do not want to interrupt your reunion."

"Nonsense. Besides we were discussing you."

"Were you, indeed? Do tell." She took the seat next to Luke and the men returned to theirs.

"Yes, I was just expressing my wish to meet you," Philip said.

"And here I am. What brings you back to England? You were not injured, I hope?" she asked, placing her napkin across her lap and selecting a piece of toast.

"No, I come on war business."

CHAPTER 17

*T*wo days passed with no word from Lady Amelia. She had not been seen walking in the park, and Meg had received a short, hastily scrawled note from her, stating her uncle had made excuses for her to stay inside and there were now guards posted discreetly at every exit. Meg was beginning to worry and that made Luke worry. Then that morning, Hawthorne had sent his regrets for the betrothal dinner.

Luke was also growing concerned, but he had not thought of another plan to get Amelia out of Hawthorne's grasp safely or, preferably, legally.

"Why the frown?" Meg asked as she entered his study looking lovely in a simple dove grey lutestring. "I knocked several times," she said, apparently feeling shy.

"You are welcome anywhere in this house." If only she would allow herself to relax, Luke thought. She still worried for her sister, with good reason. He stood and came around his desk to stand beside her.

"I cannot sleep. I feel I must do something other than enjoy the luxuries of your home."

"And I think I must call on your uncle or, better still, meet him in public." He handed her the note he had received that afternoon from Hawthorne, declining their attendance.

Luke would have given anything to erase the expression of horror from her face.

"What are we to do now?" she whispered.

He stepped closer, wanting to wrap his arms around her and comfort her. "I do not know," he answered honestly. "Hawthorne's guard is up. If I thought it would be possible, I would take her from his house with whatever force necessary, but we must try to do this the right way first."

Tears were pooling in her eyes and Luke could not bear it. Pulling her up against his chest, he reflected he would ask forgiveness later. She seemed to melt against him, however, and he relished the feel of her. This was where she belonged. Could he convince her in time? She still seemed inclined to resist more often than not.

Stroking her hair and back, he felt the moment when it happened —when she surrendered. Those eyes looked up at him, so dark from her tears he felt himself falling deeper and deeper under her spell. For what else could explain his behaviour?

"Forgive me, Luke," she said, though she stayed where she was. "I fear I am taking advantage of your honour."

"Nonsense. I am a gentleman, of course, but this I do, my lady, not only because it is right, but because I wish to."

"Truly?" she asked, still looking up at him.

"When will you trust me?" he asked, lowering his lips to hers. He was taking advantage, but he must use all tools available, it seemed, to convince her he wanted her. His heart ached as he pulled her closer into his embrace, the pleasure of her lips smooth beneath his own and yielding to him with a warm response. Her arms wrapped around his neck, and when she let out a faint sigh of pleasure, he almost lost control of what was to be a simple kiss.

· · ·

A SLIGHT SCRATCH on the door was the only warning they had before the intrusion. A servant would not have entered without his command.

"Forgive me," Philip said as he paused his forward motion. "I did not realize you had company."

"Saving me from myself, it seems," Luke muttered as he stepped away.

Meg stepped back but did not leave. "Have you news, Captain?" she asked.

"A little," he confessed. She sat on the edge of a chair so they could also be seated.

"Major Blake and his man both set sail on the first invalid ship from Bilbao on the twenty-third of June. That boat reached Portsmouth eight days later."

"How many days to Humberside from there?"

"At least a week in the best of conditions, riding straight through, I would guess."

"So it is possible, then. Our war-horses are trained to such distances."

"I am afraid so," he said, flicking a glance at Meg to see her reaction.

"This is a good thing, is it not?" she demanded. "We were hoping for something to use against him. My parents cannot be returned to me, and if he is, in fact, guilty then I wish to see him hang."

"Bravo, my dear." Luke applauded her bravery.

"I still wish there was more proof. When do you speak with Prinny?" Philip asked.

"On the morrow. I would wager that the threat will be enough to allow for some concessions from Hawthorne. I only wish to make our Regent aware should something worse happen."

"A wise move. I requested all of the documents listing the offences against Major Blake, should you need them."

"Is there nothing I can do?" Meg asked softly. Those glorious eyes wavered between them, watching the interchange between Luke and Philip.

"I know it is hard to be patient, but we must not provoke him any more just yet. He has already had his plans disrupted."

"Has anyone spoken to Erskine? He may be no more in the know than to be seeking a fertile young wife in the quest for the elusive heir," Philip said by way of suggestion.

"True enough. It was all over the betting books. I have not heard word from Thurgood either."

Meg stood up anxiously moving around the room. The two men rose to their feet in polite response. She waved them back down.

"I cannot agree with waiting, your Grace. I am convinced he has already made plans."

"How can I discover what those plans are if he refuses to meet with me?" Luke asked.

"Perhaps I should call on him," she suggested, though she was obviously not excited by the prospect if the wary look on her face were an indication.

"Absolutely not," Luke growled, furious with himself when she shrank back. "We must find another way."

She threw her hands up in exasperation. "There is no other way. He will see me."

"Much though I hate to put her within Hawthorne's reach, I must agree with her," Philip said calmly.

"I had hoped to avoid it until I have attained my majority, but it cannot be helped," she reasoned.

"Only if I accompany you, and not at his house." Luke gave her what he hoped was an uncompromising look.

"It may be however you wish," she responded, flushing a little, "but we must be prepared."

"I would only suggest you speak to Prinny before Hawthorne." Philip paused. "And take Lady Margaret with you. She will touch him in ways you cannot."

Luke hated the thought, but Philip was right.

∼

MEG DID NOT KNOW why she was so terrified. She kept telling her self the Prince Regent was just a man, but even in the far reaches of her small village, people rejoiced in every small tit-bit of gossip about the future sovereign. Meg was being presented at court, in a way, but was not required to wear the formal attire expected for a court presentation.

Lady Laurence was also in the party, to pay her respects to Queen Charlotte, so the whole affair seemed sanctioned.

Again, Meg was wearing a borrowed gown from Luke's sister, one that was suitable to be in the presence of royalty. It was more garish with flounces and lace than she would choose for herself, but she had to admit she looked well in the lavender silk.

There was a soft knock upon the door and Susie opened it. Luke was standing there dressed in his finery, though not full court regalia. Meg had never thought pantaloons and Hessians so attractive, not to mention the dark blue coat that looked especially tailored to his form.

She rose and sank into a deep curtsy. "Your Grace."

He moved to stand before her and extended his hand to help her up.

She took his hand, laughing. "I suppose that was a bit too deep."

"Never fear, Prinny will be charmed. I am prepared to fight him for you."

"Do not be ridiculous."

"You wait and see. Prinny has a soft spot for beautiful women, though you are rather young for his taste." He held out a velvet pouch, which he opened to reveal a parure of sapphires and diamonds.

Meg gasped eagerly as she reached out to touch the precious jewels. She had seen her mother wear such things on rare occasions, but Meg had never worn anything more than pearls or her locket.

"May I?" he asked.

Before she could answer he was already removing her locket. The touch of his fingers on her neck caused her skin to prickle. She was suddenly more aware of him and acknowledged that she was becoming accustomed to the sensation of what she presumed was desire. She looked up to see Susie had discreetly left the room. Meg was both grateful and alarmed. Luke had always been a gentleman—it was still gentlemanly to kiss, was it not? She had overheard conversations between the maids and knew things could go beyond kisses. However, would he think it acceptable to do more if he thought in their minds they were to be married?

As if answering her questions, she felt his warm lips on her neck, where his fingers had been moments before. Was he intentionally trying to scramble her wits? It was a very effective method, and suddenly the warnings from her governess and mother made much more sense.

"Forgive me, you have a beautiful neck," he said, not sounding at all repentant.

"That is not a compliment I have heard before," she retorted weakly.

He laughed, his lips still on her neck, and she felt the deep rumble inside. She must find a way to distance herself from him, for she did not know how long she could resist him. He was temptation in every sense of the word.

"Luke... Luke," she repeated more firmly, finding her voice. "We must go."

"Yes, of course." He fastened the necklace as she placed the earrings in. He settled the tiara upon her head and stepped back to admire her. "Fit for royalty, I believe."

Meg smiled. It really was dangerous to be so close to him. He would be tempting whether he was a Duke or not.

They began to walk downstairs to meet his mother for the short ride to St. James's.

"How have you managed to avoid the parson's mousetrap so far?" she asked.

He laughed. "Thankfully, there are not too many young ladies and mamas willing to follow the drum in order to catch a coronet."

"Though there are some?"

"Yes, there are some. Wellington has his own court, of sorts, and he does enjoy a fine ball. In fact, his officers must be good dancers."

"Then I shall look forward to a dance with you."

He lifted her hand and kissed it tenderly. "You may have as many as you like, my dear."

A throat cleared from the stairs and Luke greeted his mother. Meg hid her face. Whatever must she think of her?

"Are we ready to go? We must not keep their Highnesses waiting."

The butler held open the door and they hastened through a cold rain to their waiting carriage. They were travelling in full state, with the Ducal crest and four liveried footmen. There had been a few times Meg had travelled in such a manner with her family, but it was not often a display of that grandeur was called for at their country estate.

She sat next to Lady Laurence and Luke sat in the forward seat across from them. His long legs touched hers and the space seemed small with him in it. Would she always feel his presence so strongly?

She tried to halt her thoughts. She could not think of the future with him. She still must let him go. If they found their way together when they were not under duress, perhaps she would consider a marriage with him. Who was she trying to fool? Any candidate for her hand would be unfairly weighed and measured against him, but he was as close to her ideal as she could imagine in any human.

Remaining quiet, she became lost in her unproductive thoughts. Luke and his mother exchanged comments, but she paid them no mind. All too soon, she was being handed down from the carriage and escorted into the Palace.

Lady Laurence was shown in a different direction, and Luke escorted Meg into a waiting chamber. Having heard of the Prince Regent's bent towards the extravagant, she was unsurprised by the gilt ornamentation surrounding her. Plush red carpets lay underfoot and bold paintings covered the walls in the overwarm room. Before long, a bewigged servant in Royal livery escorted them into another chamber.

Meg was not prepared for the onslaught of charm, in corpulent abundance, before her. She curtsied deeply and Prinny was immediately standing in front of her.

"My dear," he said as he reached out and took her hand. "You have my utmost condolences for the loss of your parents."

"Thank you, Your Royal Highness."

"Waverley." He acknowledged Luke, who bowed.

"Your Royal Highness."

The Prince tucked Meg's hand under his and began to walk about the room with her. She cast a sideways glance at Luke, who looked part amused, part irritated. He mouthed *I told you so* and she almost giggled.

"Waverley has told me of this situation with your uncle. If true, I am most displeased." He looked towards the Duke and back to Meg. "You may speak, Lady Margaret."

She smiled sadly. "I am not privy to what he told you, but my uncle did sell me to an American merchant, for a great sum, without my consent. I was drugged when I did not acquiesce and I awoke on a ship. I was barely able to make my escape."

The Prince frowned. Had she said the wrong thing? In person, he did not seem frivolous at all to her. Was the public perception of him wrong?

"He also has plans to wed my young sister to Lord Erskine, but that is not criminal."

"What of your parents' deaths?" He looked at Luke, but she answered.

"My instinct tells me it was no accident, Your Highness, but I have no proof."

The Prince was still frowning but continued to lead her about the room as if on promenade in front of a grand crowd. Perhaps he was a creature of habit. Luke followed quietly behind.

"I am not well acquainted with the new Marquess, other than faint recollections of him being an annoying lad. Nothing suspect has reached my ears before I received your note, Waverley."

Luke stepped forward so as not to be speaking to the Regent's back. They stopped and faced one another.

"Unfortunately, I was acquainted with him in the army. He was not an officer to present the Kingdom's interests well." Meg thought that was stating the situation rather politely but she held her tongue.

"I see." The Prince released her arm and placed his hands behind his back. He began to walk in a circle, deep thought etched on his face. Apparently, he interpreted Luke's statement accurately. He was much sharper witted than rumour had told of him.

Luke stepped closer and spoke softly, most likely for the Prince's benefit so he might think her delicate ears were being protected. "I suspect there may be a more nefarious purpose to Hawthorne than his efforts to profit from his nieces' beauty."

"The devil, you say?"

"Wellington sent Elliott here to investigate possible connections."

"Why have I not been told? Warned?"

"If we brought every offence directly to you, we would be short of men on the field." Luke smiled. He knew how to handle the Prince well, Meg reflected. He was quite diplomatic.

The Prince made a noise of acknowledgement, but a scowl pulled at his features.

"Send Elliott to me. I want a direct report." The Prince had made his decision and the frown was gone. He returned to the charming rogue and smiled, his attention all apparently on Meg.

"You are officially betrothed, now, I hear?"

"Yes, Your Highness," she replied meekly, not daring to speak the whole truth.

"I am delighted you saved her, Waverley. Can't have our beauties being taken over to the rebels, eh?"

"I agree completely, sir."

"An excellent match. I am quite jealous." The Prince sighed. He had neatly walked them back to the door. Taking Meg's hand, he kissed it almost seductively. She saw Luke straighten, but he kept quiet.

"It has been delightful, Lady Margaret. I look forward to dancing with you at your wedding."

Meg dropped into a curtsy. He turned to Luke with a quite different personality. "I want to know every development, the second it happens."

Luke bowed. "Of course, sir."

Meg's mind was swirling. There was more information regarding her uncle's deceit than she had known. Why had Luke kept it from her? They walked behind a footman to another part of the palace, and she kept from voicing her thoughts until they were alone. They waited for Lady Laurence in another beautiful anteroom and were served tea while they waited.

"I know you have questions," Luke said quietly. "I will answer them when we return home."

Home. The natural way he said it made her insides turn warm. She gazed at him over her tea-cup, trying to be angry with his high-handedness. There was no way in which she could release him from a betrothal after that royal edict and he knew it! Why was he doing this?

Giving her a roguish look, his eyes twinkled as if he could read her thoughts. She would not consider how they could have a conversation without words, for it would distract her too thoroughly. Instead, she considered the tea tray and plucked a tiny cake into her mouth, daring him to try her further. He only looked amused and relaxed back into his chair. She was in trouble, indeed.

CHAPTER 18

*L*uke had had enough. He wanted to speak with Hawthorne and have everything finished. He had possibly been presumptive in speaking to the Prince before the Marquess, but it was clear Hawthorne wanted to be difficult, if not dirty. It would be almost comical if Hawthorne agreed to Luke's terms when they met, but he had no expectations of such gentlemanly consideration. For one, he had not responded to requests for meetings. In fact, Luke assumed the only reason the Marquess had sent regrets to the betrothal dinner was to be spiteful.

Tobin had finally happened upon the information that the new Hawthorne preferred Brooks's to White's, so Luke had decided to force the conversation. The Marquess would not dare snub him as a duke in public.

Meg's father had been known to frequent White's on the rare occasions he was in Town, so it was no surprise the usurper had different preferences. Luke spoke quietly to the major-domo and was directed to a dark room that smelled of smoke and spirits. There was a deep game of cards going on and Hawthorne was in the thick of it.

No surprise there, he thought wryly.

Luke discreetly looked around the room and spied Philip in the corner observing the proceedings. He gave him a slight nod, acknowledging his presence, and then settled his attention on the scene before him.

Luke was socially acquainted with all the men present, but was close to none of them. He had joined the army and they had stayed behind as peers or heirs to protect their titles and sew their oats. They were the epitome of bored, rich men on the town.

Luke took a seat behind the crowd which had gathered, meaning the stakes were high. Luke recognized young Amberley and wondered what he had risked. His nerves appeared about to shatter as his hands shook and sweat dripped down his brow. Hawthorne looked ready to devour the young pup. What was his purpose? He had the Marquessate and the wealth, so what other game was afoot?

Staring at the man, he was fair and striking. The ladies had favoured him, even without the title, due to his looks and uniform. Meg had even said she had not suspected anything duplicitous in his nature before. Was this a recent change, then? He would study the records on him when he returned home.

Amberley tentatively played a card at last, and Hawthorne's eyes gleamed with victory. What kind of man enjoyed destroying others in such a fashion? *A heartless one,* he replied silently, answering his own question.

Luke waited until the crowd dissipated. Amberley signed over the deed to a property, and Luke clenched his jaw with disgust.

Hawthorne still had not noticed Luke. He stepped forward then, while there were enough people still present, so the snake could not avoid him without making the snub deliberate.

The Marquess looked up as he began to leave the table. Luke spoke first.

"Hawthorne."

"Waverley."

Luke caught the first glimmer of fear in the man's eyes. Good, let him worry. "I would speak to you in private, but since you have declined to answer my requests, shall we speak here?"

A few men turned back at Luke's tone of voice, to see if something interesting was about to ensue. Excellent. Luke wanted people to be suspicious.

"I believe this could have waited until an appropriate hour, but if you insist." Hawthorne held out his hand towards two chairs in the corner of the room. Philip stayed where he was, which was as planned.

"Let us have done with the pretences. I cannot imagine why you wish to speak with me."

"Can you not? I never took you for a dull-witted man, merely a selfish one."

"Are you trying to force me into a challenge?"

Luke pretended to ponder the idea. "Perhaps that would be the simplest way to have done with this affair. If I thought you would behave as a gentleman, I would do so. I would like an explanation for your treatment of your nieces, if I must spell it out for you."

"Not that it is any of your concern, but I have done no more than arrange excellent marriages for my wards," he drawled lazily, although Luke was sure his eyes missed nothing below the hooded lids.

"Then you will not object to our marriage. Unfortunately, Lady Margaret was already promised to me when you arranged the affair with Mr. Thurgood."

"I knew of no such arrangement. Please convey my apologies to dearest Meg. I wish you joy. Besides, it is not my fault Thurgood could not manage to hold on to her. Our bargain was completed when she arrived on the ship."

Luke chose to ignore the shrewd way the blackguard worded Meg's boarding of the ship. "I am sure you will not object to our visiting with her sister, then."

"Now, there you are mistaken, your Grace." He almost sneered. "I must protect my younger ward from the dangers of this world."

"And you consider my future duchess, your niece, a danger? You are seeking a challenge, indeed."

"I am doing no such thing. Can you argue that your future wife did not run away? Would you like it bandied about that she was on her own, unchaperoned, for more than a week? I have witnesses."

"Would you like it known that you drugged your niece and planned to wed her secretly to a cit?"

"Tush, tush. There is no proof of any such thing. Meg always was wont to overstate the case."

For perhaps a second, Luke stared at the vile creature. As the leer widened, he swung his fist and planted Hawthorne a facer brutal enough to draw his cork. The Marquess staggered backwards, crashing over a chair as Luke shook his hand. No doubt he had broken a couple of fingers... and it was well worth it.

Luke stepped forward and stood over the man, waiting to see if he would retaliate. Hawthorne glared through the one eye that was not already swelling and darkening. Philip came up close behind for support.

"You are a bloody fool," Hawthorne growled.

"Upon my honour, you will pay for this." Luke and Philip turned and left him on the floor, blood dripping down his face.

MEG PACED the Persian carpet in the study for what felt like the thousandth time. She knew Luke had gone out, and she was worried about him. They had not had a chance to speak of the afternoon's revelations and she was growing more worried by the moment. It was almost five o'clock in the morning and he still had not returned. Finally, when she had talked herself into resting in a chair by the dying fire, she heard the front door open and she ran to the entrance. Luke looked exhausted and she shrank back into the room behind her, but too late. He had seen her.

"Meg. Did you sit up?" Luke asked as he shed his greatcoat and beaver hat, placing them on the table in the hall.

"I was concerned when you did not return for dinner." She felt ridiculous, voicing her fears aloud. What a country bumpkin he must think her! Suddenly she wished she had gone to bed.

"I had some business that needed tending to." He took her arm, led her back into the study she had just vacated and stoked the fire.

"Nothing serious, I hope." She sat down and watched his profile as he worked.

"The Archbishop wrote to warn me that your uncle has requested a special licence at Doctor's Commons."

"He did what?"

"It seems he plans to wed your sister to Erskine quickly and quietly. He told the bishop that it was out of respect for her being in mourning. The bishop declined due to her age and my note of warning. He is afraid Hawthorne will go to someone else—who will be more understanding for coin—though he did promise to send word to the other Archbishops to deny the request if made."

"Oh, Luke! What can we do?"

"I am sorry I have failed you. I am not giving up, but I may not be able to prevent her marriage to Erskine. At least the man is old and is unlikely to be able to harm her. She would also, in all probability, be able to marry again soon, before her youth has passed."

"No! I will not accept it!"

"Your uncle knows we are suspicious. I spoke with him."

Meg could only stare.

"He has no intention of allowing you to see Amelia. Perhaps when she is wed to Erskine and he has what he wants you will be granted leave to visit."

"There must be a way!" Meg cried, and within a heartbeat found herself wrapped in Luke's arms. There was little more to say that had not already been said. She inhaled deeply, and was comforted by the warmth of his body and his delicious scent of vetiver... until her stomach decided to growl. Meg was mortified. "I did not feel like eating much with you not here."

Luke began to shake with laughter. "Shall we feed you, my dear?" He led her to the kitchens and sat her down at the table where she had spent hours preparing food only days before.

He then disappeared to pillage through the pantry, returning with his arms full of ham, cheese and bread. While she sliced some meat and cheese, he set the kettle on the range and found a teapot.

"Am I interrupting?" They both looked up to see Tobin, wearing a smug expression.

"You look like the cat that got the cream. What have you been up to?" she asked.

"What I do best." He smirked.

"I presume you did not come here to brag about your exploits in front of my future duchess." Luke narrowed his gaze.

"This has nothin' to do with my exploits. *Gommeril gobsh—*"

The Duke cleared his throat loudly and the kettle began to bubble and steam.

"Pray tell, Tobin." Meg interrupted the male posturing. *Gentlemen of all stations could be so infuriating*, she thought. She stood up to make the tea, but Luke waved her back down and poured the water over the leaves.

"I found out that Hawthorne intends to bring *La Glacier* to the masquerade tomorrow."

"*La Glacier?*" Meg questioned.

Luke explained. "She is the most desired French woman in living history. She is a legend among army men on the Continent, and men of all languages throw themselves at her wherever she goes."

Tobin humphed. "She does not give any one the time of day, that one, especially the English. Why Hawthorne?"

"Cupid's arrow?"

"People like Hawthorne and *La Glacier* do not bother with such emotion, if they even have hearts."

"True. Perhaps she is the key to the mystery."

"What mystery?" Philip asked, walking into the kitchen and helping himself to a hunk of cheese.

Tobin repeated the news he had overheard in the tavern.

Philip whistled dreamily.

"I take it she is very beautiful?" Meg asked wryly.

"She is almost your equal," Philip answered promptly with deft diplomacy. Meg laughed at the absurdity.

"There is something about her which drives men wild. She makes men to do things they would never ordinarily consider," he explained.

"Such as treason?" Meg asked.

"*Beggorah*, tha' must be it!" Tobin exclaimed.

"I must send orders to have her investigated. If there is a connection to Hawthorne, it will be easier to find in France." Philip's mind was already considering. "How did you discover she was here? I cannot think Hawthorne would be so bold as to go to Paris with the war raging. She was not a refugee."

"His man cannot hold his drink," Tobin said as if it were a capital offence. "He began braggin' after two pints of ale about his master's conquest."

"Fascinating," Philip whispered.

"I kept plyin' him with ale, hopin' he would squeak more beef, but he went down too fast. He'd be laughed out of the village in Ireland."

"Perhaps, next time, move a little more slowly," Luke suggested. "I want to know if he is in debt. He seems to be amassing substantial winnings and properties since his return."

"The property Amberley lost was on the Dover coast. It was not entailed." Philip selected another piece of cheese with some ham, and took a bite.

"Perhaps Erskine has a similar property. I will have Graham look into it today."

Meg was pondering quietly as she listened and observed the men. Her mind had drifted on to other urgent concerns, mainly how to rescue her sister. No one else seemed to think Amelia's case as desperate as she did.

"I wish to go to the party," Meg pronounced when there was a pause in the men's conversation.

"It would not be proper." Luke was looking at her, his head to one side and his eyes questioning.

"I want a chance to speak with him. I will not reveal my identity to anyone else."

Everyone was quiet while Luke tapped his fingers on the table. "What if he chooses to announce your presence?"

"I will be well disguised. I think I can prevent it happening. Nevertheless, as you say, would he publicly ruin the name of Hawthorne?"

"Before, I would have said no, but he is playing with fire by bringing a known French sympathizer into England. I cannot predict his next move."

"Speaking of that little matter, I left his records in your study. Scanning through them, it appears his descent began about six months ago. Before that he had no complaints against him other than what I would consider poor officership."

Tobin grunted with disgust.

"We need someone there to look into things. Someone we trust."

"I will go myself." Philip announced.

"You have only just arrived!" Luke protested.

"Ah, but I still wear the uniform, my friend. I could not stay here long. I have other news for Wellington and I can more safely transmit the orders in person."

"I would prefer you to send someone else, Philip. I need you here to help me deal with Hawthorne."

He pressed his lips together. "Perhaps you are right. However, I am not certain there would be an adequate replacement."

"I could go," Tobin offered.

"You are no longer under oath."

"That could be changed," Tobin suggested. "Who else knows the situation as I do?"

"Are you certain you can keep a clear head?"

Tobin scowled at Philip; for a moment, Meg thought the Irishman would hit him.

"Wha' would ye do if it had been ye?" His brogue was thick with emotion and Meg held still.

Philip inclined his head and relented. "Your French?"

"Not as good as my Spanish, but passable."

Philip glanced towards Luke who gave a slight shrug of his shoulder. "He is correct."

"Very well, then let us make our way to the War Office to make arrangements first thing in the morning. I have your authority to do whatever necessary to see him on his way?" he asked Luke.

"Of course."

"You will need to dress and behave as a gentleman in case you are captured."

"Easy enough." Tobin scoffed haughtily in perfect imitation of an English aristocrat.

"Might as well buy him a commission." Luke laughed. Meg walked over to Tobin, taking his hands. "Thank you for everything you have done for me. Please be careful." She reached up and kissed each of his cheeks like a sister would her brother.

Tobin blushed. "Take care of my master," he whispered to her. She nodded, feeling tears well up in her throat. She did not like to think of what tragedies could befall this rascal to whom she had become attached.

CHAPTER 19

*W*hy did I allow you to talk me into this?" Luke asked, as much to him self as to Meg. They rode in the carriage to Lady Crewe's costume party and the plan was for Meg to alight a street ahead in order to arrive separately from them.

"You have your dagger?"

Meg padded a place where it was tucked inside her bodice.

"And the whistle?"

"I am prepared for battle, your Grace," she teased.

Emitting a long-suffering sigh, he relented. "I admit your disguise it is quite good."

"Thank you. Susie is a very adept maid. I would not have thought to disguise my hair with kohl."

"The mask shields the colour of your eyes better than I had hoped," Lady Laurence added.

"Promise me you will not confront your uncle alone." Luke did not approve of this plan whatsoever.

"I will do my best." She did not promise, Luke noticed, but truly he could not hope for more when he could not sit in her pocket without giving her identity away.

He would have preferred to have Philip shadow her, but Philip thought it more pressing to see if he could free Lady Amelia from Hawthorne House while he was occupied at the party. Luke fully intended to be seen as himself so no one could suspect him if Amelia went missing.

The carriage stopped a street before the line of carriages and Meg quietly slipped out. She would be followed closely by a footman, but Luke was still uneasy. She would reach the party much faster on foot than they would in the carriage.

By the time Luke and his mother climbed the steps to Crewe House, there was already a great crush of people and he could not see Meg.

Since it was a costumed party, there were no arrival announcements. Most disguises were anything but, his own Henry VIII no true disguise. Luke nevertheless consoled himself with the reflection that no one knew to look for Meg in the first place. His mind was still full of the beautiful picture she had presented. She had taken liberties with the famous Queen of Egypt's Cleopatra costume by fashioning a blue linen, tube-style dress and placing bangles on her arms. The entire ensemble was complemented by leather-strapped sandals. Her maid had darkened her hair, then topped it with a gold headdress with a cobra at the centre, while a narrow black mask was the final touch to conceal her identity and add a hint of the exotic. Cleopatra's power over men was legendary, and Luke now understood why. In that costume, Meg had had a similar effect on him.

Quickly scanning the crowd for his Egyptian queen, as well as for Hawthorne and *La Glacier*, he detected none of them.

"You cannot just stand there glaring at everyone, Luke," his mother scolded. "Since you did not bother to disguise yourself, you will have to mingle."

She was right, but he was in no mood to be congenial. Moving forward, he greeted a shepherdess and her sheep; a short, plump Queen Elizabeth and a Viking with very hairy legs.

Spying Lady Crewe as an apropos Mother Goose, he decided to ask her if she knew where the parties he sought might be.

"You kept your word," she said approvingly.

"Have I ever not?" He raised his brows and bowed over her hand.

"I know it is not your preferred gathering, but I am glad you came."

"Congratulations, it is quite a crush," he said as he scanned the throng.

"Who are you looking for, your Grace? Perhaps I can be of assistance."

"I had some business with Hawthorne. I heard he might be here."

"If so, I have yet to see him. The only person I cannot identify is the Cleopatra. She indicated a marble column across the room, where Meg stood alone. How he would like to go to her! A Roman centurion approached her and asked her for a dance, Luke presumed, for she shook her head. He almost sagged with relief. It was ridiculous, this notion of possessiveness he felt, but until they were safely married, he was not convinced she would not try to run away.

Despite himself, he began to make his way closer. Fighting the press of bodies caused Luke to grow warmer and more claustrophobic by the moment. Why had he agreed to come? He could not adequately protect Meg here, and he loathed crowds.

Alas, there were blessings and curses in not masking his identity.

"Excuse me, your Grace…"

"Pity about the injury, your Grace…"

"Have you been introduced to my daughter, your Grace?"

He gave a polite answer, the daughter in question being of advanced years with a tendency to smack her lips when she spoke. Had they not seen the engagement notice in the paper? It was supposed to deter the matchmakers, yet they only seemed more desperate. He was tempted to yell 'fire' in an effort to clear a path, but by the time he finally escaped Lady Middleburg's clutches, Meg was nowhere to be seen.

Trying not to panic, he was frankly rude to several people who tried to stop him. He pushed his way past groups of bewigged and masked revellers, narrowly avoiding a glass of punch, before he spied her on the garden terrace, speaking to a knight.

Stopping himself before he made a scene, he went out of another door at the far end, trying to stay out of her companion's sight. If it was Hawthorne, where was his famous mistress? Who else would Meg have gone alone onto the terrace with?

He strained his ears to hear, but they were speaking quietly.

"'Tis a clever disguise, niece."

"I needed to speak to you about my sister."

"You forfeited that right," he growled.

"For refusing to marry the man of *your* choice? How dare you drug me and kidnap me in order to have your way!"

"A good girl would have cooperated. Your sister is a very good girl." He was taunting her, and Luke had to restrain himself from ridding the earth of the man here and now.

"You would not dare!" Meg stood looking up at the man who stood a full foot taller.

"You little fool, of course I would. I already had plans for the money Thurgood gave me for you. He wanted to marry a title very, very badly. Fortunately, I have a spare to oblige."

"You will not get away with this!"

"I already have, my dear." He reached out and chucked her under the chin like an indulgent a child.

Luke thought Hawthorne was bluffing, but he could not be certain.

Her uncle laughed, a devilish sound, and walked away, leaving Meg looking defeated.

When Luke was sure Hawthorne was gone, he went to her side. She collapsed into his arms and sobbed.

"We must go after them!"

"I will leave word for my mother. I am certain she may seek a ride with one of her friends, or borrow Lady Crewe's carriage." He led her through the milling horde to the entrance where latecomers were still filing in. He found his driver himself, so there was no mistake, and requested him to meet them at Waverley Place as quickly as possible. They began to walk, since it would be some time before the carriage was able to manoeuvre through the traffic.

"Do not lose heart. We will not give up."

"I hope Captain Elliott finds her before it is too late. Do you think he has taken her to Portsmouth?"

"I should think Thurgood would want to ensure marriage before sailing, this time. If the Archbishop of Canterbury would not grant him a special licence, you would have to try one of the others."

"York? Winchester? Durham?"

"Who can tell? I prefer to find Philip and see if he has discovered anything before we chase all over England. By that point, it could be too late."

Meg was holding her composure well, though he knew it must be difficult. Luke assumed that this was a distraction from Hawthorne's greater purpose, but he had no proof nor clue of what it was.

Entering the house, Luke started barking orders as if he had never left the battlefield. He desperately wished he had Tobin and the other brethren here to help him fight Hawthorne. One thing was clear, he had to be defeated once and for all.

~

MEG HAD TO DO SOMETHING. She had waited, and to what purpose? Her vile uncle had simply traded Amelia for her.

Nothing mattered but finding her sister. They would escape somewhere, no matter what happened, and hide from the world if necessary. She went to her chamber and Susie was there, waiting to help her from her costume. As she changed her clothing, she did her best to think with a clear mind, something she had not had the luxury of when she had found herself on board a ship and leaving harbour. Trusting Luke would discover Thurgood's whereabouts quickly, she knew she must be prepared to act. It might even be necessary to kill Thurgood to get to her sister. Was she prepared to do such a thing? *Only as a last resort*, she answered truthfully. She fingered the hilt of the dagger Luke had given her. Thurgood was a large man and would not be easily overcome, so she would have to make sure she caught him unawares.

So many thoughts went through her mind. Where had he taken Amelia? When had they left? Was she afraid? Of course she was. Her uncle must have threatened her to gain her compliance.

Meg made an inarticulate sound, protesting her uncle's coercion of Amelia.

"I cannot remove the black from your hair without washing it, my lady," Susie said apologetically.

"Oh." Meg returned to the present with a jolt to find the maid standing beside her with the water jug, soap and a towel. "Leave it as is, please. It might still be useful."

Impatient to return downstairs, Meg rose as soon as she was presentable. Heedless of being observed, she hurried down the main staircase to Luke's study to see what, if anything, he had discovered. When she entered, Philip was already there and he appeared agitated. He was pacing the carpet in front of Luke's desk, recounting a story.

"I do not see how my men could have lost them!"

"You are certain they took the Dover road?" Luke asked. He appeared to be gathering something from his desk. Meg looked closer and realized it was a set of pistols.

She had to put a stop to this foolishness. "I will go," she announced. "I cannot let either of you risk yourselves for this. It is my affair."

"This," Luke emphasized, "is most certainly our business."

"I do not know how she could have escaped unless she was disguised."

"*La Glacier?*"

"Yes, she left on Hawthorne's arm to go to the masquerade," Philip replied.

"Can you be sure it was really her?"

"She was in disguise…" Philip slammed his fist down hard on the desk. "It was all an elaborate ruse!"

"Do you mean he sneaked Amelia out whilst pretending she was his mistress?" Meg asked in horror.

"And delivered her to Thurgood before coming to the party. Hawthorne was alone."

"My men did not follow him to the party," Philip said with evident self-disgust.

"You could not know, Philip, but I want you to keep eyes on Hawthorne. I suspect he is playing a very deep game. I will go after Thurgood. They could not have gone too far for they left just before the party."

"Hawthorne will not escape me."

"I am prepared to leave as soon as I hear word as to which direction they have gone. I sent men to all the principal roads from Town."

"What if they left by the river?" Meg asked. "He is a shipping merchant."

Luke looked up, panic crossing his face. He ran to the door. "Timmins, has the carriage returned?"

"Yes, your Grace, Thomas has it ready for you."

"I will search the docks."

"I am coming with you," Meg stated, afraid he would argue.

Instead, he ushered her out of the front door and into the vehicle, barely pausing for a footman to fetch a cloak. Philip was already on his way after Hawthorne.

Meg closed her eyes and prayed they would catch them before it was too late.

"I still think Hawthorne will try to marry your sister first, but you are probably right about the docks. He could be married on board the ship, but it would not be recognized here in England."

Meg remained silent as the carriage negotiated traffic and wove through narrow streets and around warehouses. She was too distracted for words. The smell of the river reached them before she saw any water. "Let it not yet be high tide," Luke muttered, but Meg's nerves were too overset to speak, and she had likely shredded the trim on her pelisse from fidgeting with it.

Meg knew very little about sailing, but she did know the tide was when large ships could leave the harbour. It was what had saved her the first time.

When they came upon the docks, Meg looked out of the window and began to panic. There had to be hundreds of ships there! Some large masted ships, barges covered with crates, and smaller ferries and skiffs congested the area near the docks.

"How will we ever find them in time?" she cried. "They all look alike!"

"The larger ships going to America are at the West Indies docks."

"They are organized?" she asked with hopeful surprise.

"To some extent. Smaller ships are scattered where they can find a berth."

The carriage drew to a stop. "Wait here," he directed before he stepped out. She could hear him conversing with someone, although she could see very little from the small window. It must be the busiest port in the world—and a fine place to kidnap someone if ever there was one! The people she could see paid no mind to anyone around them; sailors were going about their business and porters were loading cargo onto ships.

Instinct told Meg Amelia was on a ship, but would she have gone willingly or had she been drugged? Would Thurgood take another chance at marrying into the English aristocracy?

Footsteps approached and Luke opened the door.

"We have time," he said calmly. "The tide is not in for a few hours. However, no one seems to know who Thurgood is or if he has business here. It could take some little while."

"I will help you look." Meg moved forward to alight but Luke stopped her. "This is no place for a lady. I know I am not having much luck myself, dressed as I am. I sent a few urchins out to ask, but we need more men."

"How long would it take to send to Bow Street?"

"Not long at all. We can go ourselves." He directed the driver and climbed back into the carriage.

Luke allowed Meg to come inside with him. Sir John Fielding was the director of the Runners and Luke was shown directly to him. Luke succinctly explained the situation and Sir John called for several men to join them and repeated the story for the six men, directing them to search the docks. He also told them to take a good look at Meg so they might recognize her sister. She blushed under the scrutiny. "Her hair is a beautiful copper colour, but our looks are otherwise similar."

When the Runners had left, Luke led her back to the carriage.

"What now?" she asked.

"We return home and wait."

"I was afraid you would say that."

CHAPTER 20

*A*fter they had returned home, Meg sat in the window-seat in the drawing room overlooking Mount Street and did not say a word. It was as if silent vigil could will something to happen faster. Luke knew from experience that watching and waiting only made things worse, but he had learned from years in the army. He doubted he could interest her in a game of cards.

"Will you have tea, my dear?" he offered.

"I do not think I can."

"You must maintain your strength. What if we have to go after her? You will be no good to me or her if you are fainting from fatigue or hunger."

She looked up at him with so much pain in her eyes it was palpable; more than anything, he wanted to share it for her. He would not offer trite reassurances now; they did not help. There was a very real chance Amelia was lost to them forever.

Even so, he wanted to accept the blame, to relieve the burden on her thin shoulders, but he knew it would do no good. He would not be surprised if Meg could not see past the weight of responsibility. She did, however, accept his offered hand and walked with him towards the tea tray, which had been brought in a few moments ago. She sat on the edge of the sofa and, with obvious reluctance, forced herself to eat and drink.

Admiring her resolve to be strong for her sister, he hoped the ordeal would be over with quickly, although finding Amelia was only one hurdle. Bringing Hawthorne down would be a more difficult one, and would very likely ruin her family name as well as resulting in the title being rescinded.

"Three of my men returned earlier, reporting no sign of Thurgood on the Bath, York, or Brighton roads. I sent them back to Portsmouth, since that would appear to be his main stage of operations from England." Luke relayed the reports he had received.

"It still leaves the London docks." Meg's voice was quiet and considered, yet she jumped when they heard the knocker at the front entrance. Following a pause, there was a tap on the study door and a Runner, named Williams they had met at Bow Street, was shown in by a footman. Luke glanced at Meg. She was perched forward, her eyes on the man; her face had gone deathly pale and she was gripping the edge of her seat so hard, her knuckles were skeletal white.

"Your Grace." The man bowed at the waist. "Thurgood does not have a ship at the London docks."

"You are absolutely certain?" Luke flicked his gaze from the Runner to Meg, whose eyes were wide with astonishment.

"I checked the registers myself, although we did look at each ship."

"Have you any other ideas of where they might have gone?" Luke asked.

"His offices are in Portsmouth, your Grace. However, one merchant swears he saw one of his ships at Dover."

"Dover?" Meg questioned.

Luke strode from the room, calling for the butler and his secretary.

"Send to the stables and have the travelling coach readied for a long journey, if you please!" he instructed Timmons. Since none of the returning men had confirmed a sighting of Thurgood or Amelia on the main post roads, they must set forth at once. Meg followed him into the hall.

"This is worse than searching for a needle in a haystack!" she moaned.

"We must try to remain calm and think clearly." Luke placed his hands on her shoulders and, leading her back into the privacy of the study, attempted to reassure her. "Perhaps my last man has not returned because he has spotted them and is following. In which case, I hope to hear word soon. This is a good clue, however, and I wish to pursue it. If you prefer to remain here, I understand."

"I only wish to find her." She bit her lower lip as it quivered.

The Runner was still standing to one side, waiting for Luke's orders. "Would you like me to send more men that way, sir?"

"I would," Luke answered. "If they go on horseback and arrive at the ship before Thurgood, mayhap they can create a diversion."

"I like the way you think, your Grace." He bowed and left quickly.

Luke hoped for a miracle. It could be good fortune that Thurgood happened to have a ship in Dover, but it would also be quite a coincidence."

"You should prepare a portmanteau," Luke suggested.

"You will allow me to come with you?" Meg voiced her surprise.

"Your sister will need you. I can send for my mother, if you so wish."

She shook her head. "I do not want to delay. I will be ready in five minutes."

Luke watched her hurry away and finished his own preparations, including an explanation to his mother. They would have to travel in the dark most of the way. If Thurgood was trying to catch the tide, he had a considerable advantage over them. It would have done no good to guess a direction, however, for Luke would have chosen Portsmouth, not Dover. He did not understand why his own man had not returned or sent word. Had Hawthorne baited all of them? Was he about to embark on a wild goose chase?

Luke sorely missed Tobin. He was a clever devil and would have realized Hawthorne's plan before he himself had. He only hoped his batman would find the necessary evidence to condemn Hawthorne for good.

~

MEG TRIED to relax as much as it was possible given the situation but she told herself there was nothing she could do until they reached Dover. Luke was sitting on the seat next to her and she was very aware of his presence—and warmth—so close. His long legs consumed the limited space inside the carriage, yet instead of being fearful, she relished the security his presence provided.

As if sensing her thoughts, he reached over and took her hand in his without saying a word. They sat together, passing through the darkening town in thoughtful, but unalarmed, quiet. The buildings began to thin and the sun sailed beyond the horizon as they reached the Dover Road. When they pulled up to the toll-gate, Luke tapped on the ceiling and the carriage drew to a stop. He opened the door and stepped out.

The gatekeeper looked wary to see such a person. It was unlikely most people paid him any attention, and when they did it was not usually good, Meg suspected.

"What can I do for you, my lord?" he asked, pulling off his cap.

"We are looking for a man who has abducted my sister. They would have driven through here a few hours ago."

"You are not the first one to come past asking after a lady."

"It was probably one of my men."

"I don't know about no lady, as I told him, but there were a gent who came here in a fancy carriage like yours, without the crest. I couldn't say what were on the inside. The only other business were the mail-coach and the stage."

"Thank you," Luke told the man and handed him a coin.

Coming back inside, he took his seat. "You heard?"

"Yes," she said softly. "It does not mean it was her."

"No, but it is the most help we have had thus far."

He gave her hand a comforting squeeze and she settled her head against his shoulder. She would not have thought it possible to sleep, but when she woke, they were travelling down the hill into Dover.

"Good morning," Luke said pleasantly.

Meg felt her cheeks warm as she realized the ungraceful manner in which she was sprawled across him. No doubt she had sleep marks across her face, she thought in horror, self-consciously running her hands over her hair to smooth it.

"If I drool or snore in my sleep, please do not tell me."

"You did neither, word of a gentleman."

She could hear the humour in his voice. "Did you sleep, yourself?"

"A nap here and there. Mostly, I have been thinking of what we might find."

The carriage slowed as they made their way through the sleeping town. Peeking out of the window, there was smoke coming from a few chimneys and a few gas lights along the main road, but otherwise the town appeared to be abed.

"Dare I ask what you are thinking? Do you know what time it is?" Meg asked, hiding an unladylike yawn with her hand.

"I believe near to five of the morning."

"We have very likely missed them," she said, feeling as though a vice was squeezing her chest.

"Even though they were ahead of us, they would not have made the evening tide. We did not pass my man last night—the driver was watching for him–so I am hopeful we will find him in due course, with some knowledge of Thurgood, at least."

"I am afraid to hope."

Pulling her back against his side, he kissed the top of her head. He did not offer meaningless assurances, yet again, and she was grateful he did not feel he should placate her.

When the carriage stopped, he helped her to alight. She looked around and they were in front of a hotel. He instructed the driver to find a place to rest the horses, and he held out his arm for Meg as if they were to stroll through the park at the fashionable hour. Dover must be a safer place than London, and she was very grateful to be able to stretch her legs.

"What are we looking for?" she asked.

"I thought you would be grateful to leave the carriage. If we encounter anyone, my wife and I are waiting to catch the stage. You and I, however, are hoping to catch sight of my man. If he has followed them to the ship, he will be on the look-out."

"Do you think it will be the same ship he was to take me on?"

"Very likely. I would not think most merchant ships luxurious enough for passengers, but I confess to knowing very little."

As they walked along the wharf, Meg tried to recall any notable markings from the ship, but she had been in a great hurry; certainly not thinking she would ever see the ship again. There were several large ships she could discern, but nothing struck her memory as familiar.

"Do you happen to recall the name?" Luke was asking.

She closed her eyes and tried to search her recollections of that horrible night, but there was nothing beyond tying her sheet and blanket together and squeezing her body through a small window. She had slipped and plunged into the freezing, foul water below. Suddenly, there were the words in her mind, as clear as if they were in front of her at that moment.

"The *Nancy Jane*," she said calmly. "I remember looking up and seeing it painted on the boat."

"I do recall Thurgood mentioning that before, now that I hear it."

As they walked along looking for a ship with that appellation, footsteps approached and they both turned. Meg slid closer to Luke, who put a protective arm around her.

"Your Grace," the man whispered.

"Wally." Meg heard relief in Luke's voice. "Have you found them?"

"Aye, your Grace. I was afraid to lose them. I sent a note back. They are in the farthest ship to the west and plan to sail with the tide."

"Did you see a lady board the ship?"

"It was difficult to see who it was, but there was definitely a smaller passenger being led aboard."

"How long until the tide?"

"About an hour, they expect."

"Excellent work, Wally."

"Just doin' my job, your Grace. Wouldn't want no 'Mercian takin' my sister away neither." Luke and Wally discussed further plans, and Wally went back down to the water to make arrangements for a boat.

It was cold as Meg stood there waiting, with the wind blowing off the Channel. Ships stood tall out in the water, their masts still, waiting for orders. The boat may not have sailed, but there was still an obstacle to overcome—they were standing on the cliffs and the ship was out in the harbour.

"How are we to get to them?" she asked as Luke came to stand next to her.

"I am hoping the Runners are down on the quay seeing to it. I was going to find you a parlour at the hotel to wait at."

"No, Luke. I will go with you."

"I cannot guarantee your safety, Meg. There could be fighting…" His voice trailed off. She touched her hand to his arm. "I understand. I still want to go."

He looked deep into her eyes and she could see him debating in his mind. "I cannot deny you anything," he said, though obviously not pleased. He bent down and kissed her lips quickly before they began the descent down to the water. Holding her hand, they scampered down the steep path as the sun began to creep over the horizon as if it would be a beautiful day. *Pray it be so,* she cried in her heart.

"At least we do not have to deal with poor weather," Luke remarked. "The wind is not very strong, so that might be useful. I hope it will not come to that."

"How will we catch them if they sail?"

"There are always boats for hire. I do not keep a yacht. I have never been overly fond of the sea, other than to admire it from a distance."

"I used to enjoy boating before my parents' accident. I think it was part of the reason I did not hesitate to jump. I cannot imagine what Amelia must be feeling at the moment."

"We will have her soon."

It was a bold promise, but his voice did not hold doubt. She did not know by what miracle she had found Luke, but she could not imagine doing this all on her own. When they reached the basin, there was more activity. Meg could see movement on the closer ships, and it appeared some of them were preparing to sail.

Luke seemed to notice as well, for he moved toward the first person he saw and began to ask about boats for hire. Wally had not returned.

A fisherman pointed down the shore some distance, and they moved on. Hoof beats alerted them to the presence of a rider and they turned to see the Runner, Williams, from London approaching. He reined in when he came close and dismounted.

"I was looking for you, your Grace!" he said breathlessly. "We have hired two boats to take us out to the *Nancy Jane*, Thurgood's ship, but we will have to try to climb on board. It is not going to be easy. I do not know how many seamen he has on board, but we will be outnumbered, what with the sun being up and them preparing to sail the three-masted barque. All hands will be awake and on deck."

"We must try," Luke said. "If you are not happy to continue, I understand."

"No, your Grace, we will not give up, though none of us can swim. Forewarned is forearmed, I say. I am armed, at least."

"I can swim and I know where her cabin is." Meg held up her hand before the men could protest. "Please do not protest. I am going."

She could tell Luke was not pleased and she could see him preparing an argument, but then he seemed to resign himself.

"Very well, as long as you do not go alone. Thurgood would be away with both of you as soon as the tide turned."

"Let us not delay, then." Williams handed off the horse to a servant and led them to the fishing boats. The other men were already inside. They began a quiet heave-to in rhythm as they made their way to the ship.

"The cabin I was held in was in the bow. There was a small window from which I climbed down."

"Do you think he would keep her in the same place?" Luke asked.

"Not unattended, though Amelia would never do something so hoydenish as jump from a ship into the sea—especially not after my parents' drowned."

"Thurgood might not know that. We must assume she will be guarded."

"How do we get up there?" Meg asked, straining her neck to look upward at the daunting climb.

One of the fishermen pointed to some ropes and a ladder made from the same. "The other boat will guard the other side if they should attempt to escape."

Meg was still uncertain as she spied the side of the ship up close. She remembered the climb down and losing her foothold against the slippery side. Nonetheless, they had to try...it might be their last chance. When they approached, there were already some ladders over this side and another ship was alongside, presumably loading cargo across a gangway.

"We may be in luck. Why have some of you not tried to sneak in with the cargo?" Once tasks were assigned, Luke checked his pistol was ready and his dagger was still in his boot. He did not think this would end peaceably, but he did not fancy sailing to America at the moment, either.

The fishermen pulled their boat in front of the hull, hoping to go unnoticed. Meg had been keeping cover under a blanket, to hide her identity if anyone was looking.

"There is the window," she whispered to Luke, who indicated with a hand to direct the rowers. One man began to play with a rope and somehow climbed up to secure the ladder before coming back down.

"Are you ready?" Luke asked.

Meg nodded, though she was shaking inside.

"Psst!"

"Did you hear something?" Meg asked as she strained her neck to look up.

"Psst!"

"There!" The skipper pointed.

"Tobin?"

CHAPTER 21

*W*hat the devil is he doing here? Luke thought, although he was also relieved to see Tobin.

"Quick, Major, I'm going to send the girl down."

Before Luke fully understood what was happening, a pair of thin legs in breeches came over the side. Not that Luke spent a great deal of time analyzing his batman, but he knew his limbs were thicker than these. Then, the face that went with the legs looked down; she was clearly frightened, with tears streaming down her face. Luke stood tall and balanced himself in the boat, holding his arms high to reassure the girl.

She was trembling and seemed unable to make the climb. It struck him just how brave Meg must have been to save herself that night a mere few weeks ago. It had been such a short time, yet he could not imagine her not being a part of his life.

"Come along, Amelia, I will catch you," he said in a soft voice, hoping it would not carry to the crew.

"Amelia, come to Luke. You can trust him," Meg encouraged.

"Meggie?"

"Yes, my love, I am here. Take one step at a time."

The girl nodded and tried to take one step, but she was shaking so hard, Luke knew she would not make it. He signalled his intent to the skipper, and began to climb the ladder. He plucked her from the rope and she clung to him, her body racked with fear. His leg was still weak, but he dare not feel it now. He shifted her weight to his bad side and began the treacherous climb down the rope, using the sound side of his body to take the strain.

As Luke made it to the boat, other arms reached up to relieve him of his burden. Tobin was almost on top of them by the time they half-climbed, half-fell into the boat. Meg's arms went around Amelia at once, rocking her and soothing her with endearments. Luke cast a glance at Meg, who also looked surprised but relieved.

Unfortunately, this would not be the end of the fight; nonetheless, they had her for now and must remain alert until they reached safety. He signalled for the boatmen to begin rowing back to shore. Williams gave him a wave of acknowledgement that he had seen, just before a great fracas ensued above on the deck. Loud thuds, shouts and screams were heard—Williams had created a diversion. The man would receive a great reward for his efforts.

Wally was waiting for them with fresh horses when they returned to the pier. It all seemed too simple, really, and Luke wondered when the axe would fall. Hawthorne would know who had Amelia, and Luke did not have legal grounds to have either Amelia or Meg.

Fortunately, Meg had almost attained her majority, but Amelia was another case entirely.

Luke quickly had them transferred to a carriage once they reached the hotel. He knew Amelia needed coddling, but they could not spare the time. He imagined that Thurgood and Hawthorne would be after them with a vengeance this time.

"Tobin, I would speak with you before you go."

Reluctantly, he helped Amelia into the waiting four-horse conveyance and she went from his arms straight into those of her sister's. The poor girl was in shock. Luke's temper boiled beneath the surface, for she was so much younger than her sister in more ways than age. Who could force such a girl? He knew many men who would.

"Is there anything else you can tell me?" Luke asked his batman.

"Thurgood is headed to France. I did not get details, but I mean to follow him. He is waitin' for another passenger to sail."

"No word of who that might be?"

"Not yet, but my money's on Hawthorne. When I discovered Thurgood had Amelia, I abandoned other tasks until she was safe."

"How did you get on the ship?"

"I secured a passage; he is not cautious about his passengers, apparently," he said with a wry grin.

"I am not sure I wish to know the details." Luke shook his head.

"I did not count on yer arrival with a fishin' boat. It saved me some unpleasantness."

"Likewise. I am happy to be of service. Be safe, Lieutenant."

"I think I am going to like the sound of 'sir.'"

"As long as you do not get too puffed up with your own consequence."

"Never, sir!" He gave Luke a quick salute and disappeared down the road below the cliffs. It was fitting to send Tobin on this mission and as an officer. It was useless to caution an Irishman about revenge.

Luke climbed into the carriage and tapped on the ceiling for the driver to proceed. He sat forward, across from the two sisters. Meg was stroking Amelia's bright copper curls soothingly and the girl closed her eyes.

She seemed to be calming. They were quite a startling pair to behold together: Meg, even with her kohl-darkened hair and ice-blue eyes, Amelia with copper red hair and the same colour eyes. It was strange; Meg was the one with the more fiery personality, based on his brief glimpses of Amelia. Perhaps he wronged her—he had seen her in a stressful situation—and there was nothing wrong with being reserved.

His mind began to wander to what his next move should be. Not for a moment did he regret the actions he had taken thus far, but he was very concerned about how to proceed. For the moment, they would return to his town house, where his mother could give advice.

Hawthorne could not demand to search his home; however, he could not hold Amelia there for four years until her majority!

"Are you wishing us to the devil now?" Meg asked as Amelia slept. "I can see the burden strains you."

"How to handle it best concerns me, but never say you are a burden."

"I should take her away to somewhere safe. In little more than two months now, I will have my inheritance."

"You can have the protection of my name now." He was losing hope of convincing her, but he was too far invested in her to abandon her to her fate, regardless. A look of pain seemed to cross her face and she averted her eyes. What did it mean?

"I cannot ask even you to harbour her secretly for four years."

"I will not give up searching for proof of his wrongs. I still have hope that Tobin will uncover the truth about your uncle."

"I wish I had your faith," she whispered. Her voice cracked and she struggled to speak the words. He watched her as she looked out of the window. They said little during the remainder of the journey—it was clear she did not wish to converse and Luke needed to think of what was coming next. It was likely Hawthorne had covered his tracks well, but if there was a shred of evidence, they would find it. The Marquess had grown arrogant with his title and, hopefully, also careless.

WHEN THEY WERE SAFELY BACK at Waverley Place and Amelia seemed to have recovered her spirits, Meg finally thought to gently interrogate her.

"I cannot tell you how relieved I am to have you with me!" She smiled and sat next to her sister on a silver brocade chaise longue in Amelia's chamber.

"I truly thought I would never see you again," Amelia said, her chin quivering.

Perhaps it was too soon. "Let us not dwell on what might have been. We are here, together, now."

Amelia nodded and Meg put her arms around her for comfort.

"You are unharmed?" Meg could not help but ask.

"Yes," she whispered. "The man was vile, but did not touch me. He seemed to look at me as more of a daughter, but I do think he intended to wed me."

"I am glad he seemed to have some remnants of decency." Meg was more relieved than she could tell Amelia.

"Unlike our uncle," Amelia replied with a frown. "Once I knew to look for his deceit, it became readily apparent."

"Did you hear of any plans? Perhaps something about France?"

Amelia scrunched up her face as she pondered. "I know he threatened Mr. Thurgood to take us to France. We were waiting on Uncle's arrival to depart. Thank the heavens, or you would not have caught up to us, I think."

"And Tobin."

"Yes, he was splendid. Is he really the Duke's man?"

"Is or rather, was," she answered with an unladylike shrug. "Luke purchased him a commission and he is on his way to France to discover what Uncle has done."

"There was a woman, it seems. He kept speaking of returning to her and their plans. I overheard an argument between him and the American. Mr. Thurgood was upset and did not want to sail to France, but Uncle said it was the only way he could have me." Amelia began to cry again, which was better than being frozen in a state of shock but Meg did not want to upset her further.

"You rest now. I must go and speak to Luke about where we shall go next."

"I want to stay here." Her sister pouted, but allowed herself to be tucked into the large bed where she looked so small and fragile. Saying a quick prayer of thanks, Meg kissed her on the head as Amelia fought the call of sleep. Opening her eyes, she looked up at her. "Are you really to be a duchess, Meg?"

"No, my dear. Luke has agreed to a betrothal in order to protect us from Uncle."

"That is only because he wants you. Anyone with eyes can see how he cares for you."

"He is a gentleman, dearest. Of course he would make everyone think that."

"If you say so." She shook her head as exhaustion overtook her and she fell asleep. Meg swept away a tendril of hair that had fallen over her face, so thankful to have her sister back.

Closing the door to her sister's room, she stood in the hallway, leaning against the wall. It was time to face Luke and make him see reason. If he truly wanted to help, then he would help them escape to somewhere safe. If he would not help them, then they would be forced to leave on their own. The thought of leaving him caused a pain in her chest and a tightening of her throat that was futile to ignore. She went to her room to allow the indulgence of sorrow until she could compose herself. Selfishness was unbecoming and Luke had found Amelia for her. What right did she have to dictate his future because of his honour? No, this must be done no matter how much she wished it otherwise.

Some half-hour later, once she had straightened her clothing and tidied her hair, she went to his study where she expected he would be. The door was ajar and she scratched on the wood to seek a word.

"Enter," his deep voice commanded. She opened the door and stood there watching him. Even in his shirtsleeves, with his hair dishevelled, he was the picture of perfection to her. Finally, he looked up and smiled. Meg's insides melted. She did not know if she was strong enough to resist taking advantage of him.

He stood and came to her. "How is she?" he asked.

"Resting peacefully. She is young and resilient."

"Did anyone..." He hesitated.

"No. She is untouched." Meg answered the uncomfortable question for him.

"Thank God."

"Indeed."

He led her to the two chairs by the fire where they had sat the first night. It was fitting, she supposed, that they were here.

175

"Luke," she began with great reluctance, "Amelia and I must hide somewhere else until this is resolved."

He furrowed his brow but she continued doggedly.

"You know I am right. If you will not help us leave, then I will have no choice but to go on my own."

"That is unacceptable." He swallowed hard. "I have been trying to think of the best way to deal with this. In truth, I have no right to keep you here. He has the law on his side, illogical though it may be. I have no claim to you other than as your betrothed. If you were to marry me now, I could protect you."

"But what of Amelia?"

His silence was answer enough.

"Will you trust me with a little more time, Meg? Give Tobin and Philip a chance to discover some evidence?"

"You don't love me, Luke. I cannot ask you to enter into such a contract! You must marry to suit your inclinations, not your honour."

"How can you say such a thing, Meg? After everything..." He turned away, jaw clenching. "What else must I do to persuade you?"

The look he gave her held pain in it.

Had she offended him? Meg could see there was no way she would convince him before her uncle was dealt with.

"Very well, Luke. I will allow events to take their course and see what my uncle's next move is. However, if, at any point, I think Amelia is in jeopardy, I will do whatever is necessary to protect her."

Luke opened his mouth, probably to protest, but was forestalled by a knock at the door.

"Captain Elliott, your Grace," Timmins announced.

"Philip," Luke said as he stood up to greet his friend. "Tell me there is good news."

"I am relieved to see you returned," the Captain answered, looking as though he had just come from a hard ride, his cheeks being flushed and his hair tousled. "Do you have Lady Amelia?"

"She is safely tucked in her bed," Meg replied.

"Saints be praised," he said, throwing himself casually into a chair. Luke returned from the drinks tray and handed him a glass. Philip took a fortifying sip of the contents and began to recite his adventure.

"To begin with, there is no sign of *La Glacier*. I do believe the whole story was a ruse."

"We had surmised as much," Luke agreed.

"I managed to follow Hawthorne from the costumed party. He was rather enjoying his new-found attention and stayed longer than was wise."

"What happened next?" Meg was growing inpatient.

"He returned to his town house but left shortly thereafter, riding hard for Dover. It was easy enough to follow him as he made no effort to conceal his identity." He took a sip of his brandy and Meg began to tap her foot under her skirt.

"He then boarded a ship called the *Nancy Jane*."

"Thurgood's ship. It is where we found Amelia." Luke provided the extra information.

Philip raised his brows in surprise. "The devil, you say? I was told it was bound for Le Havre. I must follow, of course, but I wanted to let you know you are safe for the moment."

"Of course, that may change when it is discovered Amelia is missing." Meg stood up and began to pace about the room. She waved the men back into their seats when manners dictated they follow suit.

"We can only hope his business in France is more pressing than returning to search for her," Philip said. "I will send word when I know more."

"Thank you, Philip. I cannot keep you here forever. I know your duty is elsewhere, for now."

"Hawthorne is my duty for now until I find proof he is scheming treason." Philip rose again and bowed to Meg. "It was a pleasure to meet you, my lady. I apologize, for I will, in all likelihood, miss your nuptials. I wholeheartedly approve, though…if I cannot convince you to be mine?" He cast her one more rakish grin, his eyebrows lifting in a questioning, teasing look.

She shook her head. "No, Captain, I will not run away with you."

"It was worth a try." He chuckled.

"You had better leave before I call you out," Luke jested.

Philip held up his hands in surrender and made for the door. His hand reaching for the handle, he turned. "By the way, how did you get Lady Amelia off the ship?"

"Tobin did."

Philip revealed a slow smile, looking pleased. "How clever of him." He nodded and opened the door. "I think your man has found his true calling, Waverley."

"Who has found his calling?" Amelia asked quietly from the doorway, still looking half asleep. Watching Philip's face take her in, Meg bit back laughter. She cast a glance sideways at Luke, who was also looking amused.

"Lady Amelia Blake, may I present Captain Philip Elliot?" Luke made the proper introductions, although there was nothing formal about this intimate setting. Philip boldly took Amelia's hand and placed a kiss on her palm, the rogue.

"It is a pleasure to meet you, sir," Amelia said, blushing as she dipped into a curtsy.

"Philip was just leaving," Luke reminded him most cruelly. Meg was shaking with mirth.

"Oh, surely not before dinner, sir?" Amelia begged prettily, and Meg was taken aback by her sister's boldness.

"Alas, Luke is correct. Duty calls, although I would much rather stay here and gaze at your beauty."

Luke cleared his throat and Philip only smiled—playfully and unrepentantly—yet it was enough, it seemed, to capture Amelia's heart, Meg thought warily as she noticed the exchange of glances.

That Philip left most reluctantly, after holding onto Amelia's hand much longer than was proper, was evident for all to see. Amelia was similarly affected; she was still staring longingly at the door minutes after Philip was gone.

"Will you come to dinner?" Meg asked gently, understanding Amelia's thoughts. She had been through a great deal in the past few months and what harm would a little flirtation do?

"I do hope the war ends soon," Amelia murmured as she allowed herself to be led towards the dining room.

"We all do, my dear, but first we must decide how to keep you safe."

"At least it seems we have a reprieve. I pray Tobin can find some evidence quickly," Luke agreed.

"And if he does not?"

"We had better be prepared for battle."

CHAPTER 22

The next morning, Luke was closeted with his secretary, taking care of some necessary estate matters, though the problem of Lady Amelia was never far from his mind. The Runner he had left in Humberside had found a witness who had seen two men tampering with the boat, but they had been well disguised, in capes and low hanging hats, so Luke held little hope in convicting Hawthorne on such thin evidence. It would not be enough.

He did not doubt that their peace would be short-lived. During the night, he had slept fitfully, debating the best options for both ladies. The only solution he could find was sending Amelia back to Humberside. She would be safe while Hawthorne was otherwise engaged and then no one could claim Luke was harbouring her unlawfully. The plan was not without flaws, however, and he would not do so without ensuring her safety. His mother could perhaps accompany her.

"Pardon the interruption, your Grace, but this message came by post." Timmons entered the study and handed the letter to him.

"It must be from Captain Elliot. I did not expect any news so soon," he remarked as he slid his finger under the seal and opened it. It took him a moment to decipher the untidy scrawl. This script was slanted at an odd angle and was not one he recognized. It certainly did not belong to Philip.

YOU HAVE CHOSEN *the wrong man to toy with. If you do not return Lady Amelia to her guardian within eight-and-forty hours, your batman, who is parading himself as a lieutenant, will be turned over to the authorities. It seems he has taken a fancy to a French woman and has sold his soul to win her heart. Pity. There is a mountain of evidence against him. I confess it will be a pleasure to see him hang, which he should have done years ago.*

MEET AT LE GLACIER, *Étretat at noon with the girl.*

LUKE SLAMMED his fist down on the desk.

"Your Grace?" Graham asked timidly.

"Send to the docks to have the fastest possible ship hired for me. I will also need as many Runners as Sir John can spare." Luke barked orders as though his life depended on it. "Return to me once that is arranged and I will give you more orders."

"Yes, your Grace."

Luke went to find his mother, for she was endowed with good sense and would give sage advice. He found her breakfasting with Lady Margaret and Lady Amelia, and he hesitated to confide the situation in front of them.

"Good morning, Luke. What is it? Has something happened?" Meg asked.

He sighed deeply and sat in his chair. "Unfortunately, yes. Your uncle has discovered Tobin and is threatening to turn him over to the authorities as a spy."

Amelia gasped and his mother set down her fork. Meg, he noticed was as still as a stone.

"May I see the letter?" she asked.

The lack of emotion on her face worried him.

181

"It is not necessary." He prevaricated.

"I want to see the letter."

"Very well, it is on my desk. Mother, I had thought to send you and Lady Amelia to Humberside. I think it would be the safest place for her until this is resolved."

"If you think it best," his mother agreed. "They can hardly turn us away."

"Precisely, and it will be the last place Hawthorne will suspect."

"And he cannot accuse you of kidnapping her if she is at her own home."

"I will send a letter to the butler. He is an old retainer and will aid us," Meg said as he led her into his study and handed her the letter. She sat down while reading, her eyes scanning the words.

"Oh, Tobin, no!" She looked up at him with despair in her every feature. "What are we to do?"

"*We* will do nothing. I want you to return to Hawthorne Abbey with your sister and an army of men to protect you. I will sail to France, where Philip and the others will be there with support."

"It is a trap!"

"Of course it is. Your uncle has no intention of allowing Tobin to go free. This is personal and has been a long time in the making."

"Whatever do you mean?" she asked, wide-eyed.

Tobin would not want his secret betrayed, and Luke hesitated. "Tobin used to serve your uncle."

"Why do I think this is going to be worse than my kidnapping?"

"Let me simply say, that it would be very fitting for Tobin to be the one to drive the final nail in your uncle's coffin."

"As long as I may drive in one of them also," she said with quiet vehemence.

Luke's eyes met hers and he was surprised by the determination in them.

"You cannot think to leave me here when it is I who have been wronged! Besides, after all that Tobin has done for Amelia, and for me..." Her voice cracked.

"Yes, you have been wronged, and so has Tobin. I will see this to its conclusion, Meg. If anything happened to you…" He was now the one to become choked with emotion.

She reached over and placed her hand on his arm. Luke was still surprised by the reaction her touch caused in him.

"I will be well. I must do this." She looked up at him with pleading eyes, and he could not resist.

"Very well. Against my better judgement…again."

LITTLE WAS SAID BETWEEN MEG, Amelia, Luke and his mother as they made their way to the docks. Meg had to trust that her sister was in good hands with Lady Laurence, although her resolve failed her and it was a very tearful goodbye between the two of them.

There was so much at stake; Meg was having a hard time thinking clearly. Besides her sister's and her own freedom, there was her family's good name to be protected, and Tobin's life. Would it be possible to save all of them? Luke had not told her everything, she was certain, and she feared for the worst.

They said their farewells and boarded separate ships. Most of the journey took place during the night, and she passed it fitfully in the small Captain's cabin she had been given. Her thoughts were bleak and morbid, as they could only be in the dead of night, for she could see no way this situation could turn out well.

She had seen little of Luke since their departure; nevertheless, she sensed his presence on board and drew strength from it. There was nothing to do but fret and wait, and Meg resigned herself to it, praying for justice to prevail.

In the morning, as the coast of France drew near, Meg could feel the tensions rising. The extra men Luke had brought with them grew quiet and stood taller on watch, and Luke spent most of his time looking through a spyglass.

"Land ahoy, your Grace!" the Captain shouted.

Luke turned to Meg. "You will wait in the cabin for the duration.

Lock the door and do not open it for anyone else. Do you understand?"

Meg opened her mouth to protest, but Luke's face changed in a way she had not seen before. This must be how he dealt with his men when they were about to charge into battle. This would not be the time to argue for she would not win. His face was set, even obdurate. She nodded and meekly went to the cabin, which was the only room on the boat with windows, or so she had been told.

Desperately wishing she knew more, she paced back and forth as she stared through the glass, trying to see something... anything.

It was infuriating to be down here, helpless, when this was her battle to fight. She understood Luke felt a degree of responsibility, there being some history with Tobin and previous bad blood between Luke and her uncle, but none of this would have happened if it were not for her.

The coast drew closer; near enough for her to make out some cottages and shops along the quay. Were all transactions to take place on the ship? Or were they to go into land?

Soon she had her answer. Noises from above and a swift stop to the boat indicated they had dropped anchor. Did they wait here? A soft knock on the door followed by Luke's voice startled her.

"Meg? It is Luke."

She hurried across the tiny space and lifted the latch and he stepped in to the cabin.

"Do we wait here?" she asked, searching his eyes.

He hesitated before answering. "No. I am to meet him on shore." He took her hands in his. "I wanted to say that no matter what happens, you will be provided for. I wish you had the protection of my name, but I almost understand why you would not take it."

He shrugged sheepishly and she longed to pour her heart out to him. "Do not say goodbye to me, Luke. You will return." Her heart felt heavy, and she struggled to contain her emotion.

"I fully expect to and, I promise, that being the case I will put forward my best endeavour to convince you to have me. Until then, I will have to settle for a kiss."

He expected a kiss, after saying he might not return? Before she could argue, his mouth had descended to hers. He spoke to her through this melding of lips, which expressed tenderness and devotion and, dare she think, love? It was too much to comprehend. She allowed herself to pour her love into the kiss, love she did not have the ability to say with words. It was too much to hope this would turn out for the best.

Slowly, reluctantly, he pulled away and touched his forehead to hers. The smile he gave her would have to keep her warm through her lonely vigil.

"I must go. Lock yourself in behind me."

"Luke?" In desperation she called after him, although her throat thickened with her emotion. "Godspeed."

He gave a quick nod of his head and was gone. She lowered the latch after him and ran back to the window. It was torture, waiting; wondering. A small boat with six men began to row away from the ship. Once the dinghy had disappeared from sight, she sank down onto the bunk, trying not to despair, yet expecting a tortuous wait.

Not half an hour later, a loud bang, followed by the sounds of a scuffle, came from the deck. Meg shrank back against the wall and tried to think calmly. It sounded as though they were under attack! She quickly searched the cabin for a weapon, anything she could use to defend herself, while cursing Luke for leaving her behind. All she found was a full bottle of brandy.

"Of course," she muttered, just as the door crashed open behind her.

"We meet again so soon, Niece."

"Uncle," she breathed, looking up into the grey eyes so like her father's.

"Indeed. You do not look happy to see me. Were you expecting someone else?" He clicked his tongue. "I had thought you more quick-witted than that."

"Luke went to meet you."

His brows raised. "Luke, is it? Of course it is. You wasted no time ensnaring him." He walked towards her and it took all of her strength of mind not to recoil from him. He circled around her, a hawk stupe-fying its prey, as he looked her up and down. "Your Duke is very predictable. I knew he would not bring Amelia, and you are a much more valuable bargaining counter."

"Very well, take me, but leave him alone."

"You are in no position to negotiate, dear niece," he growled.

Meg resisted the urge to finger the dagger in her bodice, but she clutched tighter the bottle she held hidden in the folds of her skirts. "Will you tell me why?"

He stopped in front of her and leaned his face down so close to hers his breath, reeking of spirits, invaded her senses. The look in his eyes changed. He was not really seeing her at all. Much though she was tempted to bash him over the head, she needed answers. For a while, she did not think he would give her that satisfaction.

"You have no idea, do you?" he asked at length.

Meg shook her head, afraid any sound would disturb the precarious balance of the situation.

He stepped back and began to circle around her again.

"I shall start from the beginning." Broodingly, he looked her over once more; a flash of pain crossed his features and then he looked away. "Your mother was betrothed to me."

What? Meg wanted to shout the word, but somehow held it back.

"Yes, me—until I brought her to meet my family and she chose the title over me."

This could not be true! He was lying! Yet, nothing else made sense.

"It quite killed my soul. I was in love with her and she threw me away like dirty linen." He completed another circle around Meg, hands behind his back, the only sounds the click of his boot heels on the floorboards.

"She looked just like you." He stopped right in front of her, much too close, and lifted her chin. "Yes, but she did not possess your will." He dropped her chin and looked away as though disgusted. "I was sent into the army to be out of the way, and discovered it is far easier to gain favour with Napoleon than our own mad ruler or his debauched son."

Meg held back a gasp. Her uncle was definitely a traitor! It was one thing to know, but she had not been prepared for the repulsion hearing the words from his own lips would cause.

"It has all been simple, really," he mused, looking out of the windows.

Meg knew she should take advantage of his distraction and hit him over the head, but she needed to know more.

"When you play at the care-for-naught officer only interested in gaming and women, people let vital information slip unbeknownst. Napoleon pays for information, arms are diverted, and nieces' marriages are arranged for the benefit of both parties." His face took on a self-satisfied leer.

Meg's head shot up; unwilling though she was to react to his taunts, she could not prevent it.

"Yes, you had almost thwarted the final piece of the puzzle." His keen gaze seemed to see straight through her.

Her mind was churning trying to put the pieces together and anticipate his next move.

"You fetch quite a sum, which goes a long way towards supporting Napoleon's ambitions, and dearest Amelia's marriage provides a vital piece of land in the overall scheme."

"No!"

"No? You are right, it is tempting to exact revenge upon Waverley and his henchman for old slights but I must not be distracted from the greater victory. Come now, Niece. We must leave before your swain returns."

"Leave him out of this."

"I would be perfectly happy to, I assure you. He is the one who constantly pokes his nose into my affairs."

There had to be something more personal than bad blood between the two. It would explain Luke's continued efforts on her behalf. It was somewhat lowering when she had begun to think his sole mission had been for her honour. No matter the reason, her uncle must be stopped and she still did not know what he was planning.

"What do you mean to do now?"

His face contorted into a menacing scowl. "Finish my mission and leave your precious Duke to take the blame."

"If I help you, will you forget about Amelia?"

Hawthorne turned the full face of his evil on her, his eyes dark and evil. "And just what do you propose?"

CHAPTER 23

*L*uke watched from the dinghy as Hawthorne and some of his men climbed onto the ship. He saw a scuffle begin between the Runners and the sailors and directed his men to row back. He was taking a risk, he knew, by leaving Meg there for bait, but he also knew Hawthorne would not kill his most valuable asset. That being said, Luke had to make certain Hawthorne did not escape, either alone or with Meg. It seemed to take hours to return to the hull —hours of wondering what was happening and not being there to protect her.

All was quiet when they came alongside the ship, and Luke at once grew concerned. The hired men climbed stealthily up the rope ladder and when Luke arrived on deck, he found several men trussed like Christmas geese and others not so fortunate. He did not know which men were Hawthorne's—though none of the remainder, who were standing guard, made a move against him. Therefore, he concluded, they must be part of the ship's crew and following his orders. Although the men seemed to be of simple intellect, he had directed them to leave Meg unguarded.

Nodding to the Runners and sailors who had returned with him on the rowing boat, he crept towards the cabin. Straining his ears to hear above the ship's creaks and groans, he tried to listen for voices, or any indication of what might be going forward. He heard only silence.

Was he too late? Had he made the worst miscalculation of his entire life? A rush of anger caused his blood to pound through his body, a sensation he had only felt at the height of battle when an enemy was charging against him. Controlling his fury, so as not to make a mistake, he still felt his fingers shake with unleashed ire.

He crept forward to look through the broken door, but there was nothing to be seen. He opened it fully to dimness and the over-whelming odour of brandy.

"Meg," he whispered desperately, fearing he had lost her. The agony which shot through his heart was unbearable. He swore in pain, vowing vengeance through a torrent of dire reprisals. Then, as he turned towards the door, he caught a movement, barely more than the shifting of the shadows, out of the corner of his eye. Reaching for his dagger, he swung about, instantaneously raising the blade.

"Luke?" Meg whispered, looking up at him with red-rimmed eyes filled with tears. Her body was shaking and she dropped the dagger she had been holding on to the floor with a clatter.

A heartbeat later, she ran into his arms. He hugged her to him, relishing the feeling. It was then he noticed Hawthorne's prone body on the boards behind her.

"What happened?" he asked, soothingly stroking her hair.

"I killed him!" She sobbed the words into his chest.

"Tell me."

"He grabbed my arm. He was going to take me away again—away from...away. I-I panicked. I had the bottle in my hand and I struck at him as hard as I could..."

It was then that Luke noticed she had a dark stain on her bodice. Hawthorne's blood?

"My brave girl," he murmured into her hair. "You did what you had to do to save yourself." All he could feel was overwhelming pride in her courage and relief for the outcome—if her uncle were indeed dead. Reluctantly, he released her to check the inert form.

He kicked the lifeless body over with the toe of his boot; as Hawthorne's tall frame toppled face upwards, he groaned and his eyes rolled back in his head. Strips of petticoat, which Meg must have been holding, fell away from his head to reveal a deep gash.

"He is not dead yet, more's the pity," Luke told her as he searched a trunk. Having found a rope, he first tied Hawthorne's hands behind his back, and then his feet.

"Did he harm you?" Luke asked once Hawthorne was secure and could not return to consciousness and take them by surprise.

"No." She shook her head.

"Thank God! I cannot begin to tell you how much I feared for you. I should rather face a whole company of Boney's Imperial Guard than ever again leave you alone like that..."

In the next moment, some force drew them together, their lips meeting in a frantic desperation for reassurance. Of their own accord, his hands wandered to her back, her waist, and her arms, desperate to verify that she was whole. She seemed to realize this was neither the time nor place, and broke away, placing her head against his chest. He held her tight, unable to resist dropping the occasional kiss on the top of her bowed head. Her hair smelled sweet and she fit so well against him—as though she had been fashioned solely for him. Breathing deep of her perfume, he cuddled her in silence until he felt her relax.

"Did your uncle happen to mention his intentions?" he asked then, though it appeared she had prevented any future revelations, to judge by the size of Hawthorne's head wound.

"He told me the reasons for his actions and confirmed he has been aiding the French. He seemed proud of it. The sum he received from Thurgood was to support Napoleon's cause and he was to obtain from Erskine a piece of land on the coast in exchange for my sister's hand."

"There must be some plot brewing." Luke leaned back and tried to assimilate what he was hearing. That would have to wait until later. "Did he mention where he was taking you?"

"I suspect to Thurgood. He seemed intent on implicating you for his treasonous acts."

"But how?" Releasing her, Luke walked to the window and stood with his hands on his hips, staring out at the sea while trying to antici-pate what Hawthorne had intended to do next. Had he come from the land or a ship? Was Tobin being imprisoned on Thurgood's ship? Luke thought that would be most likely, for it provided little means of escape. He had no doubt Hawthorne intended to finish what he had started all those years ago and Luke prayed he was not too late. Mentally applauding Meg's strength of character, he left her for a moment while he climbed up the ladder to the main deck and ordered some of the men to watch Hawthorne with vigilance. Returning below, Luke then led Meg away from the reek of blood and brandy, and gathered together his remaining men.

"Where do you mean to start?" Meg asked as they surveyed the casualties on the deck. There must have been upwards of twenty bodies littering the deck, with several more walking wounded. One man had lost a hand, another an arm; across by the aft deck lay an unfortunate with a gaping hole where one eye should have been...

"I am hoping some of Hawthorne's men will provide clues now that they know he is incapacitated."

Luke walked over to where the Bow Street Runner, Williams, was standing guard. "We lost one man, your Grace," he said. "Hawthorne brought six, including himself, and three of them died. The other two are beaten, but alive. I don't speak enough French to make any sense out of them."

Luke nodded and knelt down before Hawthorne's men. One was alert and was glaring at him with his good eye, the other was a swollen mass of angry purple and red. In rapid French, Luke began to negotiate with the man.

"Your leader is captured," Luke said.

The man spat.

Was the Frenchman's belligerence directed at Luke or Hawthorne?

"You have no loyalty to him?" Luke asked hopefully.

"He is a traitor."

"Yes, he is, but he holds someone important to me. Fifty guineas, now, for information about the location of Hawthorne's main base of operation, and fifty more if his prisoner is returned to me safely."

"You will set me free? No conditions?"

"If you fulfil the agreement, yes."

"And if I say no, you kill me now?"

Luke inclined his head. "Can you free my servant?"

The man was quiet as he seemed to be weighing his options.

"Me, I think I do not wish to die in service to this scoundrel. I do not serve him, but something greater."

"If you choose to die here, it will not be for a worthy cause, but for his own personal ambitions," Luke agreed.

"I will help you only to get your man. This is the agreement, yes?"

"Yes." Luke began to pull money from his pocket, but the man held up his hand.

"After," he said. "You will see my honour first."

Luke bent down and cut the bonds from the man's wrists and ankles.

"We were expected here, I think," the man said.

"Yes. I served with him in the army and expected him to trick me." The man stood up, rubbing his wrists.

"Is my man on Thurgood's ship?" Luke expected Hawthorne had left Tobin there since there was less likelihood of escape.

"It is what he planned, but there was one hitch."

Luke lifted his brows and waited for the answer.

"The American refused. He no longer wished to cooperate and divert the munitions. When he realized he would not get the girl, he let us off the ship in the port and returned to the Americas."

Luke wanted to laugh. It seemed the conversation he'd had with Thurgood had made some impression, but now it meant they would be forced to go into France to find Tobin, and proving Hawthorne's duplicity would be more difficult.

"Very well. Where shall I take you?"

The man went to speak to his remaining partner, and then toured the dead bodies.

"We may see these men properly buried?" he asked. "You must pull anchor to move the ship in any case."

Luke nodded. He had not anticipated losing so many men. They would be unable to return their own man home in time for a land burial, and he suspected it would be more of a burden on his family. He would have to ensure they were looked after.

Meg had remained out of the way in the shadows, perhaps due to the battle scene. All over the deck there were reminders of what had transpired—barrels of spilled fish, broken spars of wood and patches of blood and gore. The sailors were helping to cover the bodies; they would bury them at sea later.

Once the man was satisfied the Captain would ensure the men were given their last rites, he directed him to sail towards Étretat.

"*Mon Dieu!*" the Frenchman then exclaimed, as though he had seen a ghost.

Luke turned to see Meg walking towards him. He smiled knowingly—she had that effect on him as well.

"*La Glacier!*"

Meg frowned.

"No, my *Duchesse*," Luke corrected. *Or she soon would be*, he thought, and he claimed her now for her protection.

The man did not appear convinced and kept throwing perplexed looks at Meg. She cast her own questioning glance at Luke but he had no explanations. He had, of course, heard of the famous French courtesan, but had never himself seen her.

There was no predicting what they would find in France. Although he was no sailor, he would have preferred to keep this in more neutral territory. Was Philip nearby for assistance? Was he abreast of the situation? How could he get word to him?

They anchored the ship off the coast north of Le Havre, in what appeared to be a private inlet. A tall abbey or monastery stood watch over the ocean from above. It looked golden as the rays of the afternoon sun shone upon the stone, a majestic sight from the ocean.

"Is that where my man is?" Luke asked, surveying the fortress.

"*Oui.* It is no problem. I will speak to my mistress," the Frenchman said with confidence.

"Your mistress?"

"You will see. Come." He motioned for Luke to follow.

"I think it best if you can bring him to me."

The man look surprised, but gave a very Gallic shrug and climbed into the dinghy with Luke's men. Meg continued to stand beside him as they watched the small boat depart for the shore.

"Do you think it wise to let him go alone?" she asked as the boat drew further away.

"I cannot protect you if I leave you here, and I refuse to risk taking you there."

"What about Tobin?"

"With Hawthorne out of the way, I believe Tobin has a better chance."

"What hold does my uncle have over him?"

"It is his story to tell." Luke answered shortly. He prayed Tobin would not have to endure such atrocities again, yet he did not think it would be as simple as sending the Frenchman in for him. It was unlikely whomever Hawthorne was answering to would be willing to look the other way. Luke was not willing to give Hawthorne up, and the French would no doubt deny any knowledge of him. It was the way treason worked... but would they play by the rules with Tobin now an officer in His Majesty's Army? Hopefully, they would not have to wait long for the answer.

IT HAD BEEN several hours since the Frenchman had gone into the fortress. Meg knew not how else to describe it. It was a castle-like edifice on the top of some cliffs; it did not look as though it were military. Her mind insisted on painting horrible images of Tobin clasped in chains, and a dark dungeon of tunnels filled with rats and snakes—and only the sounds they made to fill the darkness ahead of the unknown tortures to come.

Meg and Luke had been sitting watching the shore all day long, despite the chill wind coming off the water, for both were strung taut with fear and she knew Luke was questioning every decision he had made.

She reached over and squeezed his hand for comfort—both his and her own. She would not allow herself to think beyond now.

"I see them," Luke said at last, holding a spy-glass up to his eye.

Meg waited, knowing he would tell her if Tobin was there.

"It is difficult to make faces out from this distance," he said. "There appear to be six people," he added, his brow creasing into a frown deeper than the one he had worn all day.

"I believe their backs are to us. Someone is heavily cloaked." He lowered the glass and handed it to her.

It took her a few moments to become accustomed to looking through it but she finally found the boat. "The only face I can see is our Frenchman. He appears to be returning. Two men are rowing," she observed, "and three are idle in the middle. I cannot see their faces, and I cannot be certain one is Tobin."

She handed the spy-glass back to him and he turned away to make sure the crew was ready to receive the visitors.

"Will you please wait in the cabin?" Luke asked as he turned back and took her hands in his. He did not command her, she noted, and there was a pleading look in his eyes. "I do not know what may have been done to Tobin before we found him. Your uncle..."

"Yes, I know what he is capable of. I will go and discover if he has regained consciousness."

"I did not mean I wanted you to go to him," Luke corrected.

"It is for my own conscience. He cannot harm me, tied and with the guard present."

"As you will," Luke said and kissed her cheek before returning his attention to the deck.

Meg made her way down the ladder and went to the cabin where her uncle was being held. He was awake and sitting upright on the floor with his head propped against the bunk.

He glared at her but said nothing. She walked to him and looked down, feeling sick with anger and sorrow.

"Uncle, I am glad I did not kill you, if only because I do not have the constitution for it. However, you will not be allowed to succeed with this villainous plot."

He snarled at her, making a rasping sound with his throat.

"There is a very special corner in Hell for people who murder their family for earthly gain."

His face bore no signs of repentance and it firmed her belief that he was guilty. His face took on a distant look as he began to quote. *"In the middle of the journey of our life I found myself within a dark woods where the straight way was lost."*

"Have you no remorse at all? Quoting Dante's Inferno will not save your soul."

"Love, which absolves no one beloved from loving, seized me so strongly with his charm that, as you see, it has not left me yet. Love brought us to one death," he continued.

"Very well, then I shall not mind when Tobin exacts his revenge upon you." She turned on her heel to march away but then stopped. *"Soon you will be where your own eyes will see the source and cause and give you their own answer to the mystery,"* she retorted before returning back above to see who had accompanied the Frenchman.

Climbing the ladder slowly, she listened for voices, hoping to hear that arrogant Irish brogue. Instead, a female lilt came to her ears. Had the Frenchman brought the famous courtesan back to negotiate? It was difficult to imagine that someone who had to sell their body to survive, even if it was to a higher class of patron, would care enough to return for her uncle. He did not engender tender emotion in people. Was there something else the woman needed from him?

Meg climbed onto the deck and exhaled with relief when she saw Tobin standing there, seemingly unharmed. What she did not expect was to see Philip, and with a lady on his arm.

This must be *La Glacier* after all.

Meg stepped forward. Luke turned, and on seeing her, held up his hand. It was too late; the woman had already turned around.

"Mama?"

CHAPTER 24

*W*hen Luke saw the look on Meg's face, his heart sank. He would do anything to protect her, but nothing about this was going to be easy.

"*Non, ma chère*, I am your aunt."

"My aunt? My mother had a sister?" Meg asked in disbelief.

"As you see. It was not a connection she wished to flaunt."

"Why do we not take this conversation somewhere private?" Luke suggested.

He led Meg and her aunt down to the Captain's dining room, where a small, rectangular table stood in the centre of the floor. Philip followed behind, having paused to give instructions to the men on deck. La Glacier sat gracefully at the small table as though she were holding court. Meg sat down across from her in one of the Captain's fine chairs. Once the door had closed behind them, Meg continued to stare at her aunt.

"I simply cannot believe it!" she exclaimed. "What other family do I have of whom I am unaware? I know my grandmother was French. I remember her visiting a few times, but what else is there to know?

"Your aunt is *La Glacier*, the famous French courtesan and former mistress to Napoleon," Philip explained.

Meg gasped. "And my uncle murdered my parents for you? Did he also become a traitor for you?" she blurted out.

The woman remained cool, as though she had expected such a reaction. "I must tell you a story. You must believe I never asked for your parents to be killed. Your uncle took it upon himself—but I will return to the beginning."

Luke took a seat next to Meg. He could feel her trembling and took her hand in a vain attempt to reassure her.

"Many years ago, your father and his brother were both assigned to a regiment near Flanders where my family had fled during the Terror." The woman shuddered visibly at the memory.

Meg said nothing but sat staring at her aunt.

"We all fell in love," she said with a slight hint of emotion. "Your father and mother left the army to be married, and so that he might take up his duties as Marquess, but the younger son, your uncle, stayed in the army. My family had lost everything in the Terror, and your uncle was in no position to offer me the life I wished for."

"But Napoleon could?" Meg asked, disdain salting her voice.

"Precisely." The aunt eyed her niece with approval. "One did not say *non* to Napoleon if one was wise and I was in no position to do so in any case. We were not always lovers, but I remained true to the cause."

"And what of my uncle? How did he take the circumstance of your favours being bestowed elsewhere?"

"He understood that I could not anger my king. He always knew I would come back to him."

"So, he was your puppet and you persuaded him to betray his country in exchange for your approval?"

"Call it what you will. I had no knowledge of his murdering your parents—my sister—or his forcing you and your sister into unwanted marriages. He made that decision alone, as your guardian."

Luke felt Meg stiffen beside him. He could only imagine what force she was having to employ in order to control her temper.

"Why did you come here? Did you think to rescue your treasonous swain?" Philip asked from the corner where he had been observing the interchange with obvious interest.

"He is of no use to me now, as you well know," she answered coolly.

Philip inclined his head in acknowledgement.

"I came to see Francoise's daughter." She smiled at Meg. "I realize this may all come as a shock to you, but you are always welcome in my home."

Meg shook her head and Luke could see tears pooling in her eyes. "Why?" she asked brokenly.

"It is simple." She shrugged. "I chose the wrong brother."

Luke stared in astonishment at the beautiful woman whom, he imagined, Meg would resemble in a few years' time. He could almost pity *La Glacier*.

"You do not have to continue this life!" Meg pleaded.

Her aunt looked at her with sorrow, but shook her head. "I am afraid not, *ma chère*, you believe in your king and I believe in mine. Perhaps one day we may know peace again and I hope I may see you then. My life is here, you understand, and it is not such a bad life."

La Glacier stood up and walked around the table. She took Meg's hands in her own. "You have Francoise's good spirit," she said, and kissed both her cheeks. Then she reached around her neck and unfastened a necklace, the twin of the one Meg had left behind at the inn to pay Luke.

Meg pulled her own from beneath her gown and held it out before her. "They match," she said.

"*Oui.* Our father gave them to us." She refastened the clasp and placed the circlet in Meg's hand. "For Amelia. I wish I could have met her. Perhaps one day." She smiled at her niece. "I hope you will give her my love and help her to understand."

"I do not think I understand," Meg responded, with cool dignity.

"Perhaps in time." Her aunt reached out and lightly caressed Meg's cheek, and a tear escaped before she turned and brushed it away.

Luke looked over to Philip, who shrugged and then cleared his throat. "It is time to go."

The ladies parted and with one last look, *La Glacier* turned and walked out of the room. Swinging about, Meg sought the comfort of Luke's arms and wept.

"What will happen now?"

"Philip will take Hawthorne away to be dealt with, and your aunt will be returned to the castle."

"She will not be harmed?"

"No. It would do little good to take her prisoner. I am sure she had Philip's word before she decided to come aboard. They are long acquainted since she has been under surveillance for some years."

"And my uncle?" she asked, her pale eyes searching his.

"He will be dealt with quietly, in the hopes of preserving your family's name."

"Which is more than he deserves for betraying his country—and for a woman!"

"That is true, but of late I find I am more in sympathy with the sentiment. However, murdering your parents has no excuse."

"None. Luke?"

"Yes, my love?" He looked down to find her red eyes gazing imploringly up at him.

"I want to watch them leave."

He nodded and slowly led her up the ladder, to where the Frenchmen were preparing to send her aunt back to shore. Philip would deal with Hawthorne. Meg was quiet as they stood beside the bulwark and watched the sailors and her aunt climb into the small boat and row away.

Hawthorne was brought on deck next. He did not struggle, but retained enough spite to stop and sneer at Meg before being pushed past, trussed as a prisoner with his hands behind his back and two burly soldiers watching his every move. Meg refrained from speaking, but Luke felt her tension as she leaned heavily against him.

Hawthorne's hands were untied in order to allow him to descend the rope ladder. He caught sight of La Glacier being rowed away and, as Meg and Luke watched in horror, he foolishly jumped into the water.

"Lisette! My love!" Hysterically, he cried the words over and over, flailing his arms in an impotent effort to reach her.

"No!" Meg shrieked in simultaneity with the loud splash, rushing towards the gangway. Luke let her look, but held her firmly about the waist in case she should tumble over the edge in her anguish. To his relief, Hawthorne was quickly subdued with a knock on the head and dragged into the waiting dinghy. Twisting around, Meg buried her face into Luke's shoulder and whimpered. *La Glacier* did not even turn to look back.

THE WATER SLID out from the ship in waves that trailed behind them. Meg had remained on deck, watching the sea for hours, and the sun was now beginning to sail beyond the horizon. Part of her felt relief that she and her sister were safe, the other was sad for what had transpired. There was little fault that she could attribute to her aunt, although, in her opinion, *La Glacier* had chosen a life of luxury and power over one which was honourable. She could not fault her aunt for fighting for what she believed in, and yet, no matter how many times Meg tried to reconcile the tragedy in her mind, there was no making sense of it other than as evil. Her uncle had put her aunt and himself above all else.

Luke, bless him, had suggested they sail on to Humberside, where she could return to Amelia. He had not pressed her further about anything else. In fact, he was giving her the much needed opportunity to compose her thoughts. It was difficult to look to the future and not see Luke in it, but she still felt it was unfair to saddle him with further burdens. For long enough had he set aside his life for her.

She turned to look about her for the first time in hours, to see where he was. Much like her, he was leaning over the railing watching the water, apparently lost in thought. Standing slowly and stretching, she walked softly over to him. She leaned on the railing beside him, close enough to touch him though she dared not—she did not trust her emotions.

He looked at her and smiled. Even with the sorrow in her heart it lifted and she was able to return the greeting.

"How are you?" he asked simply.

"I do not know, to be honest. I think, when I see Amelia and the Abbey again, that perhaps it will all feel like a horrid dream."

He reached over and took her hand in his. The warmth and security, the small touch provided, reassured her more than any words could have done.

"What happens next?"

"I imagine that soon there will be a notice of your uncle's tragic death."

"And just like that, all his sins will be erased? I will be expected to mourn him," she said with disgust.

"In the long run it is for the best," he replied softly, stroking her hand.

"I know, but it leaves an unpleasant taste in my mouth. There is no justice for my parents."

"This is better for you and Amelia, however, and you may trust justice will be done in some way. Philip will see to it."

"If it were only me, I would prefer justice here and now, but I would do nothing to harm my sister."

"You have done everything for your sister. What of you? What do you wish for?" He looked into her eyes, seeking the answers.

Meg could not answer. She did not feel she had the right to hold Luke to the ridiculous betrothal they had made when she feared for her life and her sister's. "Luke, I..."

"Hush." He held a finger to her lips. "I know what you are going to try to do. I beg of you to reconsider before you speak. My feelings have not changed—that is if you ever understood my feelings at all. I know you think I believe myself honour bound to marry you. The fact is, you could call off the betrothal with little harm to yourself, but I beg you to take time to reflect. You have been through an inordinate amount of adversity and most likely do not know what you feel, but I would like to assure you that every day I spend apart from you will be the most miserable of my existence."

A sob of laughter broke free from Meg. "You wretch! How could I possibly withdraw, knowing I would condemn you to a life of misery?" She laughed. "I do not deserve to be so happy. No, my dear, my feelings for you are true."

"Then may we be married at the Abbey? I would rather not wait until you have observed mourning for your uncle."

Meg wrinkled her face in disgust.

"I hope that face was for your uncle," he teased.

She laughed as he pulled her into his arms. His lips began their descent to hers but paused before they met. "I will have your answer first, Lady Margaret."

She tipped her face up to look at him. "You are quite certain?"

"I am not sure what else I could do to convince you, if slaying dragons, racing across the country to find your sister and then sailing to the Continent to discover your uncle's whereabouts have not done it. I am quite at a loss."

She toyed with the pin in his neckcloth, turning the blue sapphire around. "I believe your sense of honour would have compelled you no matter who it was. I do not recall any dragons, however."

"Ungrateful minx! If you mean to torment me, then I will show you just what I feel compelled to do." His lips descended to hers and she understood she had only thought the first meeting of their lips had been a kiss. She felt his love in every part of her being. He told her he cherished her by the tender way he cradled her face; he taught her how he felt without the need of words. His actions were honourable and while she had few doubts he would have helped anyone, he had rescued her, he had saved Amelia, and he had taken her to expose her uncle and save Tobin. It was good to be taken care of. She might have been able to do it on her own, but thank God she did not have to! This was what vows meant by helpmeet and they had been through the worse before any better. If he wanted her like this, then how could she refuse the better?

She pulled away from the kiss before she completely lost her wits.

"Yes." She raised her eyes to his for an instant, smiling wryly.

"Yes?" he asked, adorably confused.

"I will marry you."

"I am glad you agree, for I was not about to allow you to set foot off this ship until you conceded."

She looked into his eyes to argue, but what she saw there made her pulse race.

"I think I would lose my honour to keep you."

"Then I am grateful you will not have to."

EPILOGUE

While three weeks for the banns to be called seemed like an eternity, Luke decided it would be for the best given the upheaval they had endured recently. He left Meg in Humberside to recover with Amelia, and plan a small gathering to celebrate their nuptials. He had affairs of his own to put in order, and matters to settle with the Home Office regarding her uncle's activities.

"This will ensure I behave honourably," he had said with a mischievous grin before kissing her goodbye.

Now it seemed as though she did naught but watch the drive for his arrival, not knowing exactly which day he would come. It had been precisely two weeks and four days since he had left. Surely, it could not be too much longer!

"Watching will not make him come any faster," Amelia said from behind her.

"No, I suppose not. But I do wish he would."

"And I wish the dashing Captain Elliott would be here as well," Amelia added dryly.

"Amelia," Meg said softly, "I would not put too much hope into a ten minute acquaintance, no matter how flirtatious the Captain was. He once offered to marry me instead of Luke."

"Oh, I know he is a great flirt, but he makes for splendid daydreams."

Meg groaned.

"As for that matter," she continued, "so does Tobin—Lieutenant O'Neill. Both are handsome heroes, dashing to the poor damsel's rescue," she said wistfully.

"Amelia," Meg murmured in a warning tone.

"Do not worry, Sister. I know the difference between a novel and real life."

"I am glad to hear it, for I might have to reconsider my wedding trip. I do not wish any undue burden to fall upon Lady Laurence while we are away."

"Go and enjoy your wedding trip. I promise to behave." Amelia said the words with an impish twinkle in her eye. Meg suddenly felt uneasy. Who was this girl inhabiting her sister's body? Amelia had always been meek and compliant, never wanting to ruffle any feathers or draw undue attention to herself. Meg shook her head. The events of the past few weeks were making her create mountains out of mole-hills. Amelia was just in the midst of her first girlhood infatuation; it was nothing more than that. Meg might be tempted by Captain Elliot as well, she thought with a smile, were she not completely and wholly in love with Luke.

The sound of hooves beating a drum on the drive finally came to her ears, pushing aside her musings. Meg turned back to the window, her heart beating faster in anticipation.

"Is it he?" Amelia asked, coming to her side and peering around the rose satin curtain.

"Yes!" Meg answered over her shoulder as she rushed from the room. Heedless of decorum and her unfashionable enthusiasm, she hurtled down the stairs and outside to greet him on the gravel fore-court. Throwing herself into his arms the moment he slid from the horse and handed his reins to the waiting groom, she cried his Christian name. "At last! I thought you would never come!" Luke laughed and twirled her about.

Lowering her until her toes touched the ground, but not releasing her, he then stole her lips in a particularly passionate kiss, without regard for who might be watching.

"Does this mean you missed me?" he asked at length.

"It means you shall never leave me so long again!" she answered, laying her head on his shoulder. "Must we wait three more days?"

"'Tis little more than two, my love. And yes, we must."

The final banns were read in church during Sunday service and they were wed the next morning in a simple ceremony. Only Lady Laurence, Luke's sister, Julia, and Amelia represented their families, while a few beloved household retainers came along to watch and offer support. It did not seem complete without her parents, but she knew they would have approved. Meg had set aside all mourning— just a little early—for the occasion, donning a bright jonquil silk gown with summer's roses to match placed amongst her curls. She felt like an angel, walking to greet her groom, and hoped that their union would be blessed by above.

They recited their vows in the small chapel on the hill, overlooking the abbey ruins and cliffs over the North Sea, and were greeted by sunshine and a brisk breeze off the water as they emerged as man and wife.

After partaking of a small feast prepared by the Abbey's staff, Meg and Luke set sail to the Greek Islands for a wedding trip, while Amelia departed for her own come out with Lady Laurence.

"Have a lovely trip and do not worry about us," Lady Laurence said with a kiss for each of their cheeks.

"Thank you for looking after Amelia," Meg added.

"I will be no trouble at all," Amelia assured them both.

"As long as you stay away from soldiers," Luke quipped with a wink.

Amelia looked as though she might give him a set-down, but she only managed a withering look. "I am sure I do not know what you mean, sir. However, I think I am quite safe since all of the soldiers are away at war."

"And the ones who are here are only on half pay!"

~

"I COULD GET USED TO THIS," Meg said as they stood on the cliffs overlooking the Adriatic Sea. There was a warm breeze blowing off the water, bringing with it the tangy scent of salty air.

"Yes, I could stay like this forever, Duchess-mine," Luke said into her ear as his arms came about her from behind.

"I do think it was wise of you to take me away, even if only for a few weeks."

"I thought we needed the time to get to know one another better and relax after the misfortune with your uncle."

"I do hope Amelia is not causing your mother any trouble. I would not have considered such a thing before, but she did rattle on about Captain Elliot before we left."

"It is only a harmless schoolgirl calf-love. Philip has that effect on every female he meets," Luke added wryly.

"Not me," she protested, "although I will admit I recognized his charms."

Luke let out a huff of irritation.

"Not to worry, my dear; my heart already belonged to you."

"A perfect answer," he murmured, rewarding it with a searing kiss.

"Where shall we go next? I suppose it is time to return home, even though I am not sure I will ever feel ready."

"We can take our time. I thought we would sail back towards Spain. After a few weeks on a ship, you will be happy to be back in England."

A servant, running towards them, interrupted their discussion and Luke reluctantly waited for the man to come up with them.

"What do you suppose he wants?" Meg asked with a frown.

"I am quite sure I do not want to know."

Moments later, the servant stood before them, breathless from his exertions and dirty from travel. "I beg your pardon, sir, but I must see this delivered to his Grace of Waverley. Are you he?"

Luke was irritated. They had left orders not to be disturbed. "I am he," he ground out.

The man fished a letter out of his satchel and handed it to Luke. Begrudgingly, Luke took some coins from his pocket and paid the man. For some minutes after the messenger had left, Luke beat the letter against his hand while staring out at the sea.

"Are you not going to open it?" Meg asked impatiently.

"I know it is not good news, and I do not want anything to ruin our trip."

"You had better open it and discover why they went to the trouble of finding us here. Sometimes, not knowing is as bad as knowing."

Luke eyed her warily, but with a deep sigh he broke the seal and opened the letter.

While Meg watched him anxiously, he scanned the note. The letter was from his old batman and as Luke read the familiar scrawl, his heart sank.

"What is it?" Meg finally asked, clearly not able to bear the suspense.

"It is from Tobin. He writes that the ship carrying Philip while he was escorting your uncle wrecked during a storm not long after it departed. Hawthorne's body was found..." Luke paused and swallowed hard, "...but Philip's was not."

Meg gasped. "No!"

Luke went on, "They are continuing to search for him but have little hope." He crushed the letter in his hands as he struggled to control his emotions.

"I am terribly sorry, Luke." Meg's arms went around him and they indulged in a brief communion of grief for their friend. "We must sail on home. Philip's family may need you."

"He did not have any family that I know of. No, wait! There was a sister."

"Then let us prepare to return home."

"You are certain?"

"Yes. It is our duty, and you have given me more than I ever hoped to have."

"And I feel the same way, despite the merry chase you led me on to get here!" He gave a half-hearted laugh.

"You must understand why it was so," she protested.

"All's well that ends well," he said with a still-sad smile.

"Indeed, I only wish that Philip..." Her voice trailed off as her throat filled with tears.

"Yes. It is a waste of a true hero. Something does not feel right about it, nonetheless."

She looked up at him questioningly. "What do you mean? You think he is alive?"

He shrugged his shoulder. "Perhaps it is my heart not wishing to accept the truth, but yes, I feel he is still alive."

"Then we should search for him. It is on the way home at all events."

"I am certain Tobin is doing everything he can, with Wellington's support."

"Then we will at least go and verify with Tobin."

He looked at her uncertainly.

"He would do it for you." She gazed into his eyes.

"He would also tell me he had led a good life and to let him go," he countered.

"When you have exhausted all hope, then you may do so."

That was very true. At the very least he owed Philip loyalty and honour—the brethren's pledge. He nodded his head in agreement. "Yes, *Pietas et honos.*"

PREVIEW OF THE GOVERNESS

Prologue

Bath, England 1814

*A*delaide stood in the entrance hall of Miss Bell's Finishing School for Young Ladies, feeling a similar trepidation as she had four years ago when she had first set foot inside. Then, she had worried about being accepted as an orphaned poor relation who had been sent to school to be out of the way. Now, her friends were off to partake in the London Season and she was to take her first post as a governess.

She pulled on her faded blue merino pelisse and turned slowly in the round, domed room, trying to take in everything about this place that had come to feel like home. Inhaling the scent of the lilies which sat in a vase near the door, she took her bonnet down from its hook.

"Where are you going?"

Adelaide turned towards the voice of Caroline, one of her four closest friends and room-mates.

"I thought to take one more walk," she answered softly, trying to hide the emotion building inside her as she tied the ribbons of her old poke bonnet under her chin.

"Alone?" Caroline questioned.

Adelaide lifted one shoulder. "It no longer matters. Tomorrow my reputation will be of little consequence."

"Why will you not accept my sponsor's offer and come to London with me?" Caroline took Adelaide's hand as she pleaded.

"Caro, we have discussed this. It is a most gracious offer, but I see no point in prolonging the inevitable. I would—could—be nothing more than your shadow."

"You would not!" she protested. "There is a gentleman out there who will care nothing for your reduced circumstances."

"You are a dear for saying so, but you know I speak the truth." Adelaide shook her head as footsteps sounded on the stairs.

"What is going on?" Jo asked as she and Penelope joined them in the entrance hall.

"Adelaide is going for a walk alone," Caroline announced with disapproval.

"No she is not. We will all go," Jo said decisively.

"Are you still trying to convince her to go to London?" Penelope asked.

Adelaide sighed. This conversation had been repeated every day for the past month, since she had announced she had taken a position in Yorkshire. She waited while her friends donned their cloaks and bonnets and they walked out onto Great Pulteney Street. Automatically, they headed along the street toward Sydney Gardens, where, for the past four years, they had walked every day it had not rained.

"I think it is time we accept the inevitable, girls."

"Perhaps your employer will be handsome and want to marry you," Penelope said in her typically pragmatic way.

"Do not be ridiculous, Pen. He no doubt has a wife who would object."

"It could happen." She defended her suggestion as the other girls shook their heads.

"I will keep an eye out for a rich gentleman who will care not if you have no dowry," Jo said practically.

"And I will try to find a husband who has a home in Yorkshire," Caro insisted earnestly.

"I cannot think of a husband." Adelaide interrupted their fantasies as they reached their favourite spot within the labyrinth. She stopped and turned to face her dearest friends. "And if I did happen to receive an offer, I could not marry for mercenary reasons."

"You would rather be a governess?" Caroline asked with astonishment.

"I am no Charlotte Lucas." All the girls shuddered at the thought of the hideous Mr. Collins from *Pride and Prejudice*, one of the books they had read over and over together through their years at school. "It is universally acknowledged amongst us that anything is better than marrying out of desperation."

"Of course it is!" they insisted.

"Yet Mr. Darcy is fictional."

"Adelaide!" Caro exclaimed as though she had spoken heresy.

"I do not begrudge you for going to London," Adelaide continued. "I am mostly sad because everything will change. You will all marry and move to various parts of England."

Caroline burst into tears as Adelaide struggled to contain her own desire to sob uncontrollably. It felt as though everyone else was moving on with their futures and she would be stuck in a never-ending cycle of being an upstairs servant.

"This was not supposed to happen, Addy," Jo said, dabbing her nose with a handkerchief.

"We were all supposed to go to London together and marry for love!" Caroline insisted.

Jo nudged Caroline with her elbow. "Those were silly promises we made to each other when we were children."

"I want you to keep those promises...for me. There is no reason you should all suffer."

"It does not seem fair," Caroline protested.

"If I know you have found happiness, it will make my circumstances more bearable. Then I may come to be governess to your children," she added dryly.

"Oh, Addy!" Caro exclaimed. "You must not say such things!"

"Whyever not? I am counting on it. Now, let us not be sad. It is the last night we will all be together."

"For now," Jo corrected, though Adelaide knew better than to hope.

AFTERWORD

Author's note: British spellings and grammar have been used in an effort to reflect what would have been done in the time period in which the novels are set. While I realize all words may not be exact, I hope you can appreciate the differences and effort made to be historically accurate while attempting to retain readability for the modern audience.

Thank you for reading *On My Honour*. I hope you enjoyed it. If you did, please help other readers find this book:

1. This ebook is lendable, so send it to a friend who you think might like it so she or he can discover me, too.
2. Help other people find this book by writing a review.
3. Sign up for my new releases at www.Elizabethjohnsauthor.com, so you can find out about the next book as soon as it's available.
4. Connect with me at any of these places:

www.Elizabethjohnsauthor.com
Facebook

Instagram
Amazon
Bookbub
Goodreads
elizabethjohnsauthor@gmail.com

ACKNOWLEDGMENTS

There are many, many people who have contributed to making my books possible.

My family, who deals with the idiosyncrasies of a writer's life that do not fit into a 9 to 5 work day.

Dad, who reads every single version before and after anyone else—that alone qualifies him for sainthood.

Wilette and Anj, who take my visions and interprets them, making them into works of art people open in the first place.

My team of friends who care about my stories enough to help me shape them before everyone else sees them.

Heather who helps me say what I mean to!

And to the readers who make all of this possible.
I am forever grateful to you all.